Pamela Kavanagh

Hoofbeats at Midnight

Copyright: © 2009 by Pamela Kavanagh
Cover and inside illustrations: © Jennifer Bell
Cover layout: Stabenfeldt AS

Typeset by Roberta L. Melzl
Editor: Bobbie Chase

ISBN: 978-1-934983-20-1

Stabenfeldt, Inc.
225 Park Avenue South
New York, NY 10003
www.pony4kids.com

Available exclusively through PONY.

Prologue

A breeze frisked across the paddock, stirring the grass and lifting Cobweb's raggedy mane as she grazed. I was staying with friends Kate and Tom Roscoe at their family's farm for the summer vacation – my parents being too tied up with our eventing yard to take time off. Six glorious weeks of riding lay ahead. Best of all, I had my mare back after two long years without her. Life could not have been much better.

Except for that night, my first here at Broselake, when the strangest thing happened and I was out at first light, trying to make sense of it.

I climbed over the boundary fence and scanned the area beyond, looking for signs. A trail of hoofprints leading off across the ground, a tuft of horse's hair on the bushes of prickly gorse, the turf kicked up where the rails had been jumped. Anything to prove that I was not a victim of my own wickedly active imagination.

There was nothing. Only the grazing mare, the quiet fields and beyond, the empty reaches of the plain. Behind me was the farmhouse in its muddle of yards and outbuildings. By the gate of the adjoining paddock, Kate's chestnut Arab, Zaide, and Tom's colored cob, Gold Brick, stood flicking their tails at the flies. Three horses.

Yet last night from my bedroom window I had seen four. It had been there in Cobweb's shadow – silver-gray, thickset, its mane and tail full flowing. A plains stallion, broken away from the herd, I thought.

Alarmed that Cobweb might vanish off the planet all over again, I wanted to rush out and investigate. But when I looked again she was still there. And she was alone. In the other paddock Zaide and Gold Brick cropped the grass unconcernedly under the bright arc of a new moon.

There was no gray stallion. No beat of hooves. Nothing.

I stood there in the soft light of morning, hearing the sad birdcalls and prickling all over with foreboding. Even then I refused to accept that this was one of those weird flights of fancy I was prone to, that my gran called a gift but which I had banished to the past. All that was for babies.

I had not yet heard about the moon horses.

Chapter 1

"I bet you couldn't believe it when you got that phone call about Cobweb," Kate said to me, dumping a box of grooming tools at my feet.

"You're right, I couldn't. We had other calls after she went missing, but they were all false alarms. When we followed this one through we didn't get our hopes up too much," I told her, delving into the box. I took out a dandy brush and ran it over Cobweb's flanks. Dust and hair flew out in choking clouds and Kate made a face.

"Phew! She can't have been groomed much, wherever she's been."

"She's a mess, isn't she? Mom didn't recognize her. I did, though. There's no pony on earth like Cobweb."

I stopped grooming, put my arms around Cobweb's neck and hugged her. She smelled of grass and warm, sweet horseflesh. Having her back again was a dream come true.

Two years ago almost to the day, Cobweb had disappeared. It had been during summer vacation and there was a training rally scheduled with the Sport Endurance Club I had joined. I went to bring Cobweb up from the field where she was turned out with the warmbloods my parents raised and schooled, and discovered she was gone. Instead of the rally I had so looked forward to, there was panic.

We did all the usual things one does when a horse or pony goes missing: called the police and Horsewatch, contacted the auction yards in case Cobweb turned up at one of them, put out images of her all over the Internet and photos in store windows and all the horse magazines. We even organized a helicopter search of the plains. We did everything we could to find her, but Cobweb had vanished seemingly without a trace.

I was devastated. Mom and Dad offered to get me another pony, but I was not interested. I only wanted Cobweb.

There was still plenty of riding to be had. When you grow up on a training yard you live and breathe horses. Life was not the same, though. The loss of plain, bay, sweet-natured Cobweb had left a huge gap in my existence. I never gave up hope that we would find her. And then last week the telephone call had come and there she was; scruffy, matted, yet hard-muscled and fit. It was my fourteenth birthday. I could not have had a better birthday gift.

"Two whole years." Kate shook her head wordlessly. "Where could she have been all that time?"

"We don't know. She turned up on the plain during the summer roundup. The person who called us had bought a job lot of youngsters at the auction and Cobweb was with them. The vet read her identi-chip and our name came up."

"So she could have been running wild out there all along."

"It's possible. An overhead search isn't all that reliable. You know how vast the plain is, and an individual animal would be hard to spot in a herd. Dad was afraid it was rustlers behind it all."

"Dire!" Kate shuddered. "I dread something like that happening here. We don't have high-tech security the way you do at Cotebrook. If I were to lose Zaide I'd be absolutely devastated."

"The thing is, rustling is practically unheard of on our side of the plain. We're all too well geared up for it. How she went missing was a mystery."

"She must have been spirited away," Kate said with a grin.

Maybe the moon horses took her!

The words came back to me with such force that I caught my breath. They had been spoken by an old man who lived in our village. Afterwards he had slid his gaze away, as if the idea had freaked him out. I had thought no more of it until now.

"What is it?" Kate said. "You look all funny and faraway."

"Just thinking." I shrugged, telling myself I was going overboard and, swapping the brush for a comb, I started on Cobweb's straggly mane. "We've had her checked over for injuries and so on. The vet said she was all right, but we haven't seen the full report yet. I hope it's clear."

"It will be," Kate said encouragingly. "She seems bigger than I remembered."

9

"She's 14.2 hands exactly. Mom checked with the measuring stick. She's grown a little – well, that's to be expected. She was only four when she disappeared."

Cobweb was six now. We had to do a lot of making up for lost time.

I kept on combing, holding sections of her forelock between my fingers, easing out the knots and matted ringlets, removing the grass seeds and sticky burs that were trapped in dusty harvests in the thick growth of coarse black hair.

"Zaide's 15 hands," Kate went on. "Gold Brick is about 16.1. He's big for a cob, but Tom's tall so it's not a bad thing." She was studying Cobweb, fiddling with the end of her long braid of auburn hair the way she did when she was thinking something through. "Fat, isn't she, considering? Got quite a belly on her. It must be all that plains grass she's been gorging on."

"Oh well, we'll soon work it off," I said, dragging the comb through the rest of the mane and releasing a small dust storm of nose-tickling pollen that brought on an explosive sneezing attack. "Ugh," I gasped, sniffing, eyes watering. "Grooming always does this to me in the summertime."

"Does it? You should take an antihistamine," Kate said sympathetically. She flicked her braid over her shoulder. "Did I mention Mom called the farrier to come over and get Cobweb shod up? We've got Ann Jenkins at the Ravensmoor forge now. She's really good."

"Oh great. We only got Cobweb back the day before yesterday so there hasn't been time to get her done."

"That's OK. We can get Gold Brick and Zaide shod as well." Kate broke off, frowning. "Oh, look. What's that on Cobweb's neck? There, on the crest. A mark of some sort."

"It's… nothing much," I said, combing the mane firmly back into place.

I didn't want Kate touching that mark. I didn't want anybody touching it.

Kate shrugged. "It must be scurf. Her coat's full of it. There's some really good anti-scurf shampoo in the tack room. We could try it out on her if you like."

"Yes, OK," I said.

We exchanged a grin. Kate and I were the same age. We had been friends forever. Tom was two years older. He was a natural with horses and a whiz on the guitar, anything from classical to folk and rock. I had a reasonable singing voice and the three of us had formed a band, Tom playing while I sang and Kate beat a rhythm on the drums, which she said was her thing because it came already tuned.

"OK, Cobweb. You're in for the ultimate in equine beauty therapy!"

Laughing, Kate delivered Cobweb a thumping slap on the rump and went hurrying off to get the shampoo, while I kept on grooming, my thoughts racing.

I had come across the mark hidden away under Cobweb's mane shortly after bringing her home from the yard where she had turned up. I was talking to her in her box, telling her things the way I always used to, and she had tossed her head in response, sending her long tatters of mane flying and exposing the strange circular imprint on her crest. It was a chunky little horse inside a crescent moon.

When I had gone to touch it, the way Kate had nearly done just now, I went ice-cold all over. It was as if the chilly breath of winter had reached out to me in the steamy heat of the stable and I drew back in alarm, shivering, hugging my arms around myself to fend off the vibes that seemed to be zinging all around the box.

At that moment Dad arrived, back from visiting a client, and flinging Cobweb a puzzled look I went to tell him the good news about getting her back. Delighted though he was for me, there had been an argument over bringing her to Broselake. Dad wanted to keep Cobweb at Cotebrook and do a refresher course before plunging her into the schemes Kate and I had planned.

"We'll be fine," I said. "I've been up on Cobweb and she didn't do anything silly. She wouldn't. Cobweb and I are soul mates. Anyway, you won't have the time to work with her. You and Mom have enough going on as it is."

"True." Dad gave in. "Just don't take any chances, that's all."

I had just laughed. The prospect of Cobweb being anything other than utterly controllable was crazy.

We gave Cobweb her bath and spent the rest of the day generally chilling out and talking over how we would spend the vacation. Kate wanted to do a camp ride, which sounded like fun. There was a Sport Endurance rally scheduled. Tom was interested in exploring a section of the high plain that lay to the north of the farm which was not so popular with riders because it was uncharted territory and hard on the horses.

It was evening before I got around to calling Mom – from the orchard, as it was the only area where my cell phone signal was good at Broselake.

Mom answered almost immediately. "Hi Jenna. I thought it might be you. How are things?"

"Oh, great. Mom, did you get the vet report?"

"Yes. Everything's fine. Cobweb's been given a clean bill of health. But… Jenna, guess what?"

Her voice throbbed. I braced myself for bad news. "What?"

"She's had a foal," Mom said.

I was speechless. When I had first gotten Cobweb she had been slightly big for me, and since she had good bloodlines, Dad suggested we breed her. It seemed like a sensible move, since by the time the foal was weaned I would have grown into her perfectly. We went ahead and tried to get her in foal. It just did not happen.

"I know." Mom gave an incredulous little laugh. "I was lost for words too."

"A foal," I whispered.

"Rebecca Talbot thought that running free with the herd did the trick when our more controlled attempts failed. She's the vet. She should know. It's possible, I suppose."

"I wonder what's happened to it?"

"That's anybody's guess," Mom said. "It may not have survived. Though I suppose there is a chance of it being out there on the plain with the others. The good thing is that Cobweb's fit and well. Poor girl, she's had a

13

lot to cope with, hasn't she? Is she settling in all right at Broselake?"

"Yes, I think so." I could hear a horse whinnying and figured that Mom was still on the yard. "Are you still working?"

"Just finished. I was fixing up a box for the filly that's coming in for training. The two-year-old, remember? Dad's gone to get her. I think the owner has other youngsters he may be interested in sending us. Dad's bound to say yes. You know him."

Workaholic. They both were. I was more laid back and day-dreamy. It probably drove my focused, down-to-earth parents to distraction at times.

Mom went on, "Oh well, I'd better go and rustle up some supper for when Dad gets back. 'Bye for now, Jenna. Have a great time and keep in touch, OK?"

"I will," I said.

Slipping my cell phone into my pocket, I pictured Mom in the streamlined kitchen of our large modern house, darting around to the sounds of a concert on the radio, clattering pots and flinging stuff into saucepans, every move quick and sure. It never took Mom long to get a meal on the table – or a horse groomed.

She and Dad had gotten where they were through sheer hard work and determination. Riding whatever came along when they were young, taking any tedious job available to fund a place at Equitation College where they had met, starting life together in a grim little yard where the stables were better than the living quarters. It had been a grueling climb but they had made

14

it. Cotebrook, with its well-groomed yard and stable-blocks, was their dream come true.

A foal. I still could not believe it. Was it a colt or a filly? What color? Plains stallions were usually steel-gray or roan. I pictured it at Cobweb's side, a little leggy thing with an absurd tuft of a tail and wide, innocent eyes. It would be a yearling now; taller, inquisitive, wayward. Dad said if you handled an animal well at that age it was halfway to being broken. Small chance of that happening with this one.

After a while I wandered back to the farmhouse.

Broselake – an old name meaning settlement by the water – was the exact opposite of home. A mish-mash of dark beams, secret crannies and corners, rambling corridors and twisty narrow stairs, it had been built centuries ago, and you could feel the passage of time within its walls.

"Here you are, Jenna," said Kate's mom. Meg Roscoe was in her forties but she was still incredibly pretty, with black curly hair and amazingly blue eyes. She and Mom had been friends since their school days. Our two families had always gotten along well. "Did you speak to Heather?" she asked.

"Yes," I said. "Meg, you'll never guess what."

Daniel Roscoe and Tom were sitting at the big scrubbed table waiting for their supper, and looked up expectantly. Kate, helping her Mom dish up the food, did the same.

I told them the news.

"A foal?" Tom's face split into a grin. "Wow!"

"That accounts for the slack belly on her," Kate said, practical as ever. "I thought Cobweb was supposed to be infertile."

"She was. Trust Cobweb to prove us wrong. Our vet was pretty sure it was running free with the herd that did it, when our methods had failed."

"Very likely," Daniel Roscoe said. "More natural, isn't it?"

"A foal!" Meg's eyes were misty. "I wonder what's happened to it."

"That's what I want to know. Mom thought it would have joined the others on the plain – if it survived. Some don't."

"There's no reason why it shouldn't have," Daniel said. "You should go along to the yearling roundup, Jenna. There's a chance you might recognize it. Of course, you'd need to claim it before the branding is done."

Branding.

I thought of that weird mark on Cobweb's neck. Was that what it was? A brand? All purebred plains stock bore the brands of the owners, but Cobweb was not plains bred. So branding her would be pointless.

"Yearlings all look pretty much the same," Kate said. "You'd have a hard time identifying one. Though I suppose there's always DNA testing."

"Come on!" Tom said. "You'd need to test every single one. It's just not feasible. Pity. Cobweb's a nice mare. She might have bred something good."

The two farm collies, Jess and Taggle, had come over

and were nuzzling my hand. I fondled them absently, wondering about that strange mark on Cobweb's crest and what had happened when I had touched it.

Meg put the supper on the table and we all sat down to a hearty farmhouse meal.

"I've been thinking," Kate said. "We might do some trail work with Cobweb, just to test her out."

"Good idea," Tom agreed. "If you need some muscle, I'm your man."

"You guys are just like Dad," I said. "He doesn't have much faith in Cobweb either."

"Oh, I don't think you'll have any trouble." Tom pushed a dish of tiny buttered potatoes across the table to me. "But I'll stick around just in case. OK?"

By the time supper was over and the dishes washed, everyone was yawning. Bedtime was never late at the farm, since everyone got up very early. The room I always had when I stayed at Broselake was on the side of the house, overlooking the stables and paddocks. It was an attic room, used many years ago to store apples and cheese, and was approached through a connecting door from the main landing and also by a steep back stair that led directly out onto the yard.

I fell asleep at once, only to be roused some time later by those galloping hoofbeats I had heard the night before. For a few moments I lay there in the cozy warmth of the bed, still half-asleep, listening. They seemed to be everywhere, a strange, soft thudding in the darkness. Perhaps I'm still asleep and dreaming, I thought drowsily, even though I knew I was not.

They came closer. Drumming, drumming. Wide awake now and seized by panic, I stumbled to the window to make sure Cobweb was all right. Moonlight flooded the fields. And there, in Cobweb's shadow, was the gray horse.

This time I was determined to find out more. I pulled on some clothes and shot down the back stair and out, disturbing the dogs in their kennel with my struggles with the heavy bolts on the door. They started to whine and make a fuss.

"Shh!" I whispered to them. "Jess. Taggle. Be quiet. It's only me."

I ran all the way to the paddocks, pulling up at the field gate to find Cobweb tearing at the grass with apparent unconcern. Gold Brick and Zaide looked at me in bemusement over the fence, as if they could not understand what I was doing on their patch in the middle of the night.

There was no sign of the gray stallion. Just the reeling moonlight, the dark plain, and the echo of those pounding hoofbeats in my head.

Chapter 2

"Did anyone hear a loose horse in the night?" I asked at breakfast the next morning. "Around midnight?"

Everyone looked mystified. Heads shook.

"Out on the road, you mean?" Daniel said as he buttered some toast.

"No…o. It was more like a drumming." I imitated the sound with my fingers on the tabletop. "Like it was galloping on the plain."

Kate said, "If it was a stray plains pony it would have set our group off. It does happen sometimes. One will break away from the herd and stray off. I didn't hear anything. You can usually tell if there's been a stray around. The ground gets trampled."

"I've had a look but I couldn't find anything."

"In that case it must have been the water pipes you heard, Jenna," said Meg comfortably. "Old houses are like that. You can get the weirdest noises when they're settling down at night."

I left it at that and took a piece of toast. Perhaps I was mistaken after all. It was easy to get neurotic over your pony after what had happened to Cobweb. And then Daniel ruined it all by saying, "My granddad used to say it was the moon horses going by if ever we heard noises in the night. I don't know what he meant by it. He'd never tell us."

The moon horses again. The others were all laughing.

"It was just a story to frighten you kids," Meg said.

"I didn't hear a thing," Kate repeated.

"That's no surprise," Tom said good-naturedly. "It'd take a whole stampede of horses to wake you up!"

"I don't believe in moon horses either," Kate said.

"I bet Jenna does," Tom said.

I blushed. He was right there. I saw things too, and always had. When I was very small I thought everyone was the same. It had taken school and the cruel jibes and snickers of the other children to make me realize I was unusual. After that I pretended to be like all the rest – you saw things in the flesh or not at all. I practically had myself convinced. And now the gray stallion had come along.

Kate threw a glance at the long-cased clock on the wall. "It's getting late. I'm going to fetch Zaide in. Ann Jenkins will be mad if we're not ready for her."

"I'll come too," I said.

"Stay where you are," Tom told me. "I'll bring Cobweb up for you."

Daniel and Kate left and Tom, collecting Gold Brick's head collar from the peg by the door, followed them out.

A few moments later Kate came clopping past the window on Zaide, riding bareback, her long braid of dark-red hair over one shoulder, the mare's bright-chestnut mane and tail rippling. They looked sinewy and elegant, a golden pair. Shortly afterwards Tom followed on Gold Brick. The cob was big and muscled. He had a splotchy multi-colored coat, deep-set eyes and a heavy roman nose that gave him a quizzical expression. Tom had hit on the horse's name because Gold Brick was good-hearted and rock-solid dependable, like Tom himself. People were said to sometimes resemble their pets and I wondered about Cobweb and me. We were both fine-boned and what my grandpa called brunette. When she was in better shape, Cobweb's dark-bay coat was glossy and dappled with condition marks. She had no white markings at all, which made her appear nondescript at first, though as Mom said, she always drew a second look.

From here I could see Cobweb in the paddock. She had come to the gate and was whinnying after the other horses, not wanting to be left behind. Tom put Gold Brick in his box and returned to the paddocks for my mare. Sunlight glinted on his wavy red hair, a shade lighter than his sister's, and where Kate's blue-eyed gaze was serious, his danced with merriment.

Tom vaulted the fence and approached Cobweb with his hand outstretched, the head collar hidden behind his back. All at once Cobweb jibbed violently, and flattening her ears she came straight at Tom, delivering a scything kick before swerving and belting off across the grass with her head defiantly high and tail pluming. Tom was quick, shouting and leaping sideways, and the blow aimed at him went wide.

She was coming again.

"Cobweb! No…o!" I shouted, and went charging out. Meg was at my heels and Kate came tearing from the stables. By the time we arrived at the paddock fence Tom was over it and safe. Cobweb had given the rails a splintering blow, coming to a stop a short distance away. She stood contrite, her flanks heaving and nostrils flaring, looking every bit as baffled and upset as we were.

"Phew!" Tom said. "What got into her?"

"I…I don't know." I told him. "She's never done anything like it before. It's not like her. She's so sweet."

Tom rolled his eyes expressively. "Yeah!"

"Something must have startled her," Kate said.

"Maybe it was the sun. It's very bright this morning," Meg offered. She was white and shaken. "Cobweb really meant it, didn't she?"

Just then there was the whine of an approaching vehicle and the farrier's blue van rumbled into the stable yard. Ann Jenkins got out.

"Having trouble?" she called, striding up, a youngish, capable-looking woman with big strong hands and a kind face.

"Sort of," I said. "Cobweb charged at Tom when he went in to catch her. She's never done anything like it before."

"You keep saying that," Kate said.

"But it's true," I wailed. "It was such a shock. I thought Tom was a goner."

"Huh." Ann Jenkins looked Cobweb over with interest. "Is this the mare that went missing for months

22

on end? I read about it in the horse paper. She turned up in the auction, right?"

I nodded mutely. Realization was setting in. My knees had gone rubbery and I felt slightly sick. I flung another glance at Cobweb. "What on earth made her do it?"

"It could have been anything," the farrier said, shrugging. "She may be feeling unsettled. You don't know what's happened to her these past months. She could have been ill-treated, wherever she's been."

"Surely not. Cobweb's so –"

"Sweet?" Kate finished for me. "I can think of sweeter man-eating tigers!"

"Well, she seems quiet enough now," Ann said. "You'd better fetch her yourself… you're Jenna Scott, right? Don't your folks run the warmblood yard at Cotebrook?"

"Yes, that's right."

"Then you should know what you're doing. Tom, maybe you'd better get out of the way. We'll be ready in case of problems. Go on, Jenna. Get in there."

Swallowing, I picked up the head collar, fished a pack of mints out of my pocket and entered the field.

"Here Cobweb. Mints! Come on. Good girl."

She came plodding up, mild and inquisitive as always, and thrust her soft muzzle in my palm for the treat. As she crunched it I slipped the lead rope around her neck, attached the head collar and brought her quietly out.

"Easy when you know how," Kate said, shutting the gate after us. "Hi, Cobweb. Feeling better?"

Cobweb evidently was. She went through her usual

routine, rubbing her head against us, nudging for more mints, making breathy little whickers in her nostrils. She could not have been friendlier. If she had been a cat she would have purred.

"Weird," Meg said. She threw a glance at the home field where Daniel had brought the sheep for dipping. "I have to go. The workers will be here any minute and they'll need me to work the gates. Sure you'll be OK?"

"Of course we will," Ann Jenkins said. "OK, you guys. Let's start. Can't stand around here all day. I've got another appointment after this."

The shoeing went ahead with no further trouble. At around mid-morning the farrier was packing her portable forge and tools into the van. She came over to fuss over Cobweb.

"You shouldn't worry too much about that little blip earlier," she said. "Your Cobweb was terrific to shoe. Hooves like blocks of wood, too. Exactly what you need for the endurance game."

"How did you know I was into that?"

"Tom mentioned it when I was doing Gold Brick. He said you have a rally scheduled."

"Yes, next Friday. It's just a training session. Nothing important."

"It could be what Cobweb needs to get her in sync with you again."

"That's what I thought. I wish I knew what made her kick like that. Tom's great with horses. It couldn't have been anything he did."

"No," Ann acknowledged. "In my experience if a horse or pony acts out of character there's a reason for it. You may get to pinpoint what it is if you can find out what happened after she did her vanishing act."

"It's a thought. I'll see how she does."

"Might be best. Don't worry, I've known worse. You see it all in this game." Laughing, Ann Jenkins gave Cobweb's neck one last hearty slap. "Bye, Jenna. Good luck with the mare."

After she had gone, Tom came loping up. "Hi, Cobweb. Friends again?"

Cobweb had her head over the half-door and Tom went to stroke her. But Cobweb backed off warily and went stomping off to stand at the back of the box, looking unhappy.

Tom gave his lips a rueful quirk. "So that's how it is. She's got a thing about me."

"Unless it's men in general," I said. "I'm only guessing."

"I don't know. What was she like with your dad?"

"I don't think Dad got to handle her. It was a woman who got in touch with us about Cobweb and I went with Mom to get her. There didn't seem to be any boys around at the yard, either. It could be the problem hasn't arisen before."

"Huh." Tom's face darkened. "It looks like some jerk's been giving her a hard time. Pity she can't tell us what happened."

"Ann Jenkins thought she might forget about it once she's used to being ridden again. I need to build up her confidence. Once she realizes she's not going to be hurt, she may be all right."

"True. Do you want to risk a trail ride? I'm giving Dad a hand right now but we could go this evening. It'll be cooler then. Kate is up for it."

"Me too. I'd better leave Cobweb in the box for now."

"Good idea. You might throw her some hay. It'll keep her occupied," Tom said.

I left Cobweb munching happily and went to find Kate. She was in the tack room, cleaning Zaide's saddle and bridle. Collecting Cobweb's tack, I joined Kate for a session of soaping, buffing and catching up on gossip.

✳ ✳ ✳

It was good to get away from the all-pervasive reek of sheep and chemicals and go for a ride. We went clopping along the road, passing the motionless waters of the lake after which the farm was named and entering a tunnel of lacy mountain ash, heading for the village of Ravensmoor.

"Cobweb's going well," Kate said, nudging Zaide alongside. The Arab strode out gracefully, her small, dished head tucked in, the setting sun glinting through the trees and glancing off her chestnut coat. "Is she a good ride?"

"The best." I patted Cobweb's neck. The dowsing in dermatological shampoo had worked wonders, although my hand still raised a few unsightly flecks of the oily sediment horses get in the wild to protect them against the elements. "She's got the most amazing canter. Mom thinks she'd do well at eventing, but I need to brush up on the dressage."

"I'm terrible at dressage," Tom said. He rode on Kate's other side, keeping as safe a distance from Cobweb as possible. "All those half-passes and flying changes are beyond me."

"You could do it if you tried," Kate said.

"On Gold Brick?" The cob powered along gamely, his bristly mane bouncing, his eyes wise under the floppy multi-colored forelock. A horse less suited to the dressage arena was hard to imagine. "Come on! I'm sticking with Sport Endurance."

"It might be wise," I said, checking Cobweb who had jibbed at some imagined horror in the trees. She kept it up all along the way, snorting and skittering sideways, until we came out again into the open, when she gave a relieved little snort and settled down again. Give her time, I thought. We had both changed in the years apart. We had to get to know each other all over again.

A straggle of farm cottages marked the approach to Ravensmoor. We clattered over a curved stone bridge, under which the river gurgled over brown rocks.

Traffic wound slowly down the narrow main street of the village and we fell into single file, Tom in the lead. Nothing much ever happened at Ravensmoor. It was one of those soon-forgotten places; a mix of old and newer houses, a garage with gas pumps, a square-towered church, a combined elementary school and community center, a few shops and that was about it. There was a restaurant with a swinging sign. The Mani.

Seeing it, I reined in sharply, jerking Cobweb's mouth, causing her to throw her head in indignation. "That restaurant sign. What is it supposed to be?"

The picture showed a fearsome-looking female driving a chariot drawn by a powerful gray horse against a dark, nighttime background. The driver's flowing robes and long hair streamed wildly. Loping in pursuit were a couple of wolves with sharp white fangs and glinting red eyes. Around the edge of the sign was a border, intricately worked.

I stared at it in shock. It wasn't. It couldn't be!

My heart began to thud. Everything around me, the road, the buildings, Tom and Kate and the horses, started to swim before me and recede. I felt again the icy coldness of some far-off winter, heard the echo of long-ago hooves, saw in my mind's eye the outline of a stubby gray stallion...

"The figure, do you mean?" Tom asked innocently, bringing me sharply to my senses. "That's Mani the moon goddess being pursued across the night sky by two hungry predators. The horse's name was Alsvider. It means all-swift. Good, eh? Legend has it she gets caught once in a while and that's the reason for an eclipse." He laughed. "Classic!"

"It's just a myth," Kate said. "The sign is a new one. The other one was so faded you could hardly make it out. That's why you haven't noticed it before, Jenna. Why the interest?"

28

"Oh, nothing much," I lied. My hands shook on the reins, my knees felt weak. "It reminded me of something, that's all. A… dream."

The other two looked at me strangely.

"I can think of pleasanter things to dream about," Tom said, glancing around at a sudden blast of a horn from an impatient driver. "More traffic. Why does it always happen on the narrowest parts? Let's pull in."

We waited for the car to pass, then moved on, and the awkward moment was forgotten. We were nearly through the village now. From the forge on the corner came the sound of hammering. Ann Jenkins' blue van was parked in the lot. We shouted a greeting as we jogged past, heading toward the village store that sold almost everything. It was still open, so Kate held Gold Brick's reins while Tom went in to get us ice cream cones. He came out with chocolate ice cream for us and a raspberry ripple for Gold Brick – his passion, it turned out.

"You spoil that horse," Kate said.

"So? He's worth it. Aren't you, fella?"

"Well, be quick and give it to him and mount up, or we'll never get home tonight. You may not mind being caught out on the plain in the dark, but I do. I bet Jenna wouldn't like it either."

"Too true."

We took off, reins in one hand, ice cream in the other. Trotting past a row of cottages with cars parked outside, we crossed another bridge and came out onto the first desolate stretches of the plains.

29

Dusk was drawing down as we skirted the plain. Mist rose from all the damp little hollows and high above, the moon was out. Kate and Tom kept up a cheerful banter but I was quiet. I couldn't get that restaurant sign out of my mind.

Mani. It was not so much the image on the signboard that had grabbed me, but the decorative border around the edge. It had been a repetitive pattern of a primitive-looking horse inside a curved sliver of a moon, and the spitting image of that strange, flesh-chilling mark under Cobweb's mane.

Chapter 3

That night, I heard the hoofbeats again. And there was more.

Jenna, Jenna.

"Who is it?" I said breathlessly, struggling up in the bed, rubbing sleep from my eyes.

My throat had gone dry; my heart pounded. Moonlight bathed the room and I cast a frightened glance around at the bumpy old walls and shadowed corners. No one was there. The voice that was calling me seemed to be in my head.

It babbled on, rapid and unintelligible, in no language that I recognized. I could not even tell for sure if it was male or female. And then I caught the name "Mani" and my flesh crept.

"Go away! Oh, please, stop this."

I rammed my hands over my ears to try and block the voice but it was still there, inside my head. The hoofbeats were there too, thudding, thudding. I caught the impression of tremendous speed, the flash of starlight, the horror and spine-tingling thrill of challenging pursuit. I wanted to burrow down under the comforter and hide but I had to make sure Cobweb was safe. Mustering courage,

I left the warm safety of the bed and went to the window. The gray stallion was there all right, moving with Cobweb's shadow as she roamed the paddock snatching mouthfuls of grass. She did not seem at all bothered by the intruder. It was as if she did not know he was there. But he was. I could see him.

"Get away from her!" I said on a sobbing whisper that echoed mockingly around the room. I shut my eyes tight, and when I opened them again the horse was gone. The voice and the hoofbeats were fading to nothing. Soon, all was quiet. There was just the moonlight lapping the edges of the room, and the silence.

Flinging Cobweb one last glance, I bounded back to bed and pulled the comforter over my head. I hated this weird sixth sense of mine. I wanted to be ordinary. My gran had it too. She said it was a gift and that the images and sounds never came without good reason. All I had to do was work out what the reason was.

It was a long time before I went back to sleep, and then I overslept and was late for breakfast and never heard the end of it from Tom.

Throughout the day I dreaded bedtime. I need not have worried, for nothing happened. The next few nights were quiet too. No hoofbeats. No gray stallion. No voice badgering me. I began to relax.

Daniel and Meg were out till all hours, leaving us more or less to ourselves. We decided to follow Dad's advice and worked out a daily refresher routine for Cobweb. It was very simple; fifteen minutes trotting and cantering on the lunge rope, followed by long reining on the road. Cobweb had always been bombproof in traffic. Now, when I went for trail rides out on my own she was inclined to jib if a vehicle came too close – and they invariably did. That meant I'd have to get her used to distractions all over again.

"How's it going?" inquired Ann Jenkins, coming to the entrance of the forge one day as I rode by.

"Not bad," I told her, reining in. "Cobweb's still jumpy. I wish I knew why. Something terrible must have happened to make her this way."

"Hmm. Don't you have anything to go by? Some clue, no matter how small?"

I hesitated, then mentioned the crescent moon sign on her neck, lifting Cobweb's mane so Ann could see. "It wasn't there before. It's the same as the border on the signboard of the Mani restaurant."

"Goodness, so it is!" Ann said, staring. "At least, I think it is. It's sort of fuzzy, isn't it?"

"I wouldn't say that." I gave a shrug. "It looks obvious to me."

"Well, it's got to be a brand of some sort. It isn't anything I recognize. How strange."

I smoothed the mane down again before Ann could investigate the mark more thoroughly. This was an area I avoided when grooming. I left the mane long so that nothing showed, instead of shortening it neatly the way it used to be.

"Want me to make some inquiries?" Ann asked. "I get all the horse folk here. Someone's sure to know about it."

"That'd be great, thanks. I haven't mentioned it to Kate or Tom."

"Why not?"

"There didn't seem to be any point. They think I should concentrate on getting Cobweb schooled again."

"Well, that's the main thing. Is Cobweb OK with Tom now?"

"Not really. Tom's really sad about it. He thinks she's taken a dislike to him personally."

But that was not the case.

Toward the end of the week Meg said she was going into town and asked if we would like to go along and visit a new equine mega-store we had seen advertised in the local paper. We had nothing else planned so off we went.

The mega-store was stacked floor to ceiling with all those tempting things you see in catalogues and think you might get, sometime. We came away laden. Kate had saved her birthday money and blew the whole wad on a fancy green rug with matching head collar and lead rope for Zaide. Tom bought jodhpur boots, his old ones being past their best, and some stable toys for Gold Brick to keep him amused in his box, since he got bored if he was shut in and resorted to chewing the doorframe. I bought some amazingly cheap polo shirts in black, which I had wanted for ages and which Tom said made me look ghoulish, and the ultimate in sweat rugs for Cobweb.

Broke but happy, we arrived back at Broselake to find Daniel coming out of the calf shed, empty feed buckets in hand. He was limping painfully. A little shamefaced, he followed us into the kitchen and explained what had happened.

Daniel had once had an old Moorland pony, which he used for checking the sheep when they roamed over the plain. It had died the previous year and had not been replaced. They had talked about getting a quad instead, but I think money was tight on the farm, and so far it had not happened.

Today he had wanted to check his ewes, and rather than having to make a long trek, Daniel had decided to go on one of the ponies. Zaide was strictly Kate's property; no one else was allowed up on her. Gold Brick was not agile enough for the job, so Daniel opted for Cobweb.

"What happened?" I asked warily.

"Well, she wasn't all that happy when I went into the box, but I didn't think anything of it. She's not used to me, after all."

I nodded. Daniel was experienced with horses. I knew he would never have purposely done anything to upset Cobweb.

Kate stood with lips pursed. Tom had that quirky smile on his lips. Meg looked downright apprehensive.

"After a short tussle I got the tack on her, led her onto the yard and mounted up. Talk about fireworks!"

"What did she do?"

"Dumped me!" Daniel ran his hand in bemusement over his mop of wiry gray hair. "Sorry, Jenna. I should have asked you first. I never thought."

35

"What about that sore leg?" Meg wanted to know. "Does it need an x-ray?"

"Nah! I've only got a bruise or two. And some injured pride. I've been riding horses ever since I could straddle one. Can't remember the last time I was dumped."

Tom snorted with laughter. "I wish I'd seen it!"

"It isn't funny." Kate admonished her brother. "Dad could have been hurt. It wouldn't have done Cobweb much good either."

"She'll get over it," I said quickly. "Daniel, I'm sorry. Cobweb wouldn't have done it before. Dad used to ride her when he helped with the roundups and she never acted up. I don't know what's gone wrong but she doesn't seem to like men any more."

"Oh? Not even Marcus?" Daniel said in surprise.

He knew how great Dad was with horses. The whole horse world knew there was no touch like Marcus Scott's for bringing a young or willful animal under control. I gave a shrugging sigh and told Daniel what I had already said to Tom.

"Dad didn't have much to do with Cobweb after we got her back. It wasn't long before I was supposed to come here. She'd only been in contact with women: the person who notified us about her, our vet and your farrier."

"Ann Jenkins thinks some idiot ill-treated her," Kate said darkly.

"Could be. Did she say how to overcome the problem?"

36

"Not really," I said. "Except to find out what happened to her, then go from there."

"There is that." Daniel lowered himself gingerly into a chair, wincing.

"I'll get you some arnica gel. It's the best thing for bruising," Meg said.

She went off to the hallway where the first aid cupboard was. Tom looked thoughtful. He said, "Maybe we should all make an effort to get Cobweb back on track. What if I try making a fuss over her? Let her know I don't mean her any harm."

"Anything's worth a try," I said gloomily. All the happiness of the day had dissolved. It appeared I had real problems with Cobweb. "You'll need to go easy, Tom."

"I know." Tom's eyes were full of sympathy. He had guessed what a terrible sense of disappointment I was feeling. To get my mare back and then be faced with an unexpected sea of trouble was very hard to take.

"What you need is someone like my granddad to sort her out," Daniel said. "He could whisper an animal and it never misbehaved again. He was gifted. He'd have brought your mare around in minutes."

"I don't believe in whispering and all that stuff," Kate said. She had raided the cookie jar and was perched on the table, legs swinging, eating a chocolate chip cookie. "It seems a little far-fetched to me."

"Oh, I don't know," Tom said. "It's best to keep an open mind. Our coach at school says there's more than one way to climb a mountain."

Tom was clever. He wanted to go to vet school and a have a career in equine surgery. Kate was like me. She had no idea yet what she wanted to be.

"What's climbing mountains got to do with it?" Kate popped the final piece of cookie into her mouth and fixed her brother with a hard blue-eyed stare.

"I was making a comparison."

"Oh. I'm not like you. I see things in black and white. Life's simpler that way."

"Think so? I bet Jenna doesn't."

Tom was too near the mark for comfort and I turned away. Life was never simple. It was full of twists and turns. I thought of the gray stallion that appeared seemingly out of nowhere and wondered what the link was with Cobweb and the way she had disappeared – if there was a link, that is.

"Cheer up," Tom said. "We'll fix Cobweb. Dad can toss her some hay now and then. We'll take it in stages. Nothing too pushy to begin with. We'll get her used to some good honest male sweat soon enough."

"Yuk!" Kate shunted the cookie jar toward me. "Have a handful. That's what I do when Zaide acts up. It's pure comfort."

"It'll take more than that," I said, helping myself anyway. "There's the rally tomorrow. Let's hope we get a female instructor!"

That night I had the weirdest dream.

I was in a place I had never seen before. A cliff of dark rock rose steeply to the sky, and at its foot was a deep pool of brackish water. Choking thickets of gorse and mountain ash grew all around. Apart from the plopping of the water that fed the pool, the silence was immense. There should have been birds here, the bright dance of dragonflies. Frogs and newts should have basked on the stones and the air should have hummed with insects. Instead, there was nothing. Only the waiting stillness, the stark shadow of the tall pointed rock and the silence that was so intense I could hear the hammering of my own heart.

When I woke up I could not remember the details. Only the quiet, the awful sense of desolation, and the uneasy taste of something bad about to happen.

✳ ✳ ✳

The rally was held at a farm on the other side of Ravensmoor. It was ideal for endurance riding, having a mix of pasture and thickets of tangled woodland, all surrounded by challenging stretches of the plain, with its hidden channels of peaty brown water, its patches of treacherous bog that could suck a horse under in minutes, and outcrops of moss-covered, primeval rocks.

The ride there was far enough to take the tickle out of our horses' feet and settle them down. Or so I thought. Zaide and Gold Brick arrived at the rally alert and interested, ears pricked in anticipation, but manageable. Cobweb went ballistic. The moment she saw the milling horses and ponies and felt the springy turf under her hooves, she started acting up: sidestepping, dancing on the spot, and trying to get her head down and buck. Being

shackled with a rider was no longer her thing. She wanted
the freedom of the open plain with the wind in her mane
and the ground speeding beneath her racing feet.

"Oh, stop it, Cobweb! Behave, won't you?" I
grumbled.

"She's really fired up, isn't she?" Kate said.

"Ride her around a little. She'll calm down once she
gets used to things," Tom said kindly.

The sun was out with the promise of yet another hot
day. Some of the members had come long distances and a
line of trucks and cars with trailers were parked in the only
shade available, a hedge of prickly hawthorn and holly,
bent and gnarled by the battering mountain wind. Markers
fluttered at regular intervals along the routes we were to
take, and despite my nagging unease over Cobweb I felt a
ripple of excitement. It was great to be taking part in this
again. People waved and shouted a greeting.

"Is that Cobweb?" I was asked. "You got her back!
Wonderful."

There were around twenty of us attending. We were
divided into three separate groups. It did not help that our
leader was male.

Gary Robinson, a blunt-faced man with many years
of experience in the sport, began with the usual pep talk
about conserving one's mount's energies and the need
always to make sure on long rides to carry a survival kit,
in case one had difficulties. He paused while I struggled
to bring a fidgeting Cobweb under control. She kept
pawing the ground, upsetting the black gelding next to

40

us who flattened his ears threateningly and snatched a sly nip at Cobweb's shoulder. She let out a squeal of objection and started to back up, bumping into the rider behind.

"Sorry," I said, legging Cobweb next to Kate and Zaide who were on the same team. Tom was with an older group. A very slim girl on a well-bred liver chestnut was glued to Gold Brick's side. She had dark hair cut in a perfect bob and wore top quality jodhpurs and the very latest in active-sports jackets.

"That's Cerys Paige," Kate hissed out of the corner of her mouth. "Her dad's one of the organizers. She's got a thing for Tom. She always makes sure she's on the same team as him on rallies. Pathetic!"

"She's really pretty."

"But totally un-cool. Has a cow if things don't go her way."

"Lucky for her she's not on Cobweb, then," I said, giving another nudge with my heels. Cobweb tossed her head, showing the whites of her eyes. She felt like a coiled spring. I hoped that once we got on the move she would stop this wacky performance and be the sensible mount I knew.

The talk came to an end, and we were all handed maps giving the sequence of our various rides. Our route took us across a couple of big fields, through a small wooded area and out onto the open plain, veering in a wide circle that brought us eventually back to the start. The whole ride took about an hour, which was about right for Cobweb.

Gary came across to talk. "Hi, Jenna. Good to see you back with us again. How's Cobweb?"

"She's fine, thanks."

He raised his hand to pat her. That was all it took. Cobweb went up in a half-rear, plunged sideways, and started to whirl around. Anything to avoid Gary's touch.

"Sorry," I gasped, bringing her in a tight circle and pulling up. I was doing a lot of apologizing all of a sudden. "She has this fixation about men for some reason. It's strange. She won't accept them any more."

"Really? Well! She'll have to get used to us all over again. Don't worry, Jenna. You'll get there with patience."

"I hope so. Would it be OK if I do my turn right after Kate today? Cobweb's used to Zaide."

"Sure." Gary stood back and ran a critical eye over Cobweb. "She's sweating up, isn't she? It must all seem strange to her after so long a gap. I'd take things easy today. Pull out if you need to. There'll be other rallies."

Pulling out was not an option for me. It was too much like giving up. Right from the start it had been drilled into me that you never gave up with a horse. I knew that Gary was only being considerate, so I murmured a reply and rode off to join the others at the starting post.

Cerys was there, fixing brushing boots on her horse, Merridance. She looked up, her gray eyes flinty.

"You're Jenna Scott, aren't you? I wanted to speak with you, actually. I'll be replacing Merridance after this season. I need something more challenging. One of those warmbloods you turn out at your place would probably suit me. Any chance of putting in a good word for me?"

"With my parents, you mean? I don't know. People usually make an appointment themselves and then go and talk things over with Mom or Dad. There's a waiting list for our horses."

· "That's what I thought." She gave a chilly smile, and then said, "Waiting lists only get in the way when you don't know the right people."

I couldn't believe what she was asking. My parents worked by a strict rule of thumb. Do your best for your horses and be fair to your clients. Waiting lists were never jumped at Cotebrook.

"I'll give Mom and Dad your name if you like," I said carefully, "Unless you'd rather do that yourself. You can e-mail or call the yard. Ask for Marcus or Heather. Evening's best. Mom's usually free then."

I rattled off the details, but it was a waste of time. Cerys flung me a glance of utter disdain and, snapping the remaining brushing boot on her gelding's near-fore, she mounted up and rode off without another word.

I watched her for a moment. She was one of those willowy girls with legs that go on forever, the sort that look terrific on a horse. No doubt she was a brilliant rider and gave her horse nothing but the best, but that didn't make me like her any better. All right, the way she acted toward Tom may have been a factor. She was smiling up at him now, and he was smiling down at her, absorbed in whatever it was she was telling him. All the girls liked

Tom. I suppose he was flattered to be singled out by the best looking one here.

Tom and Cerys were in the A ride, more advanced and more demanding on horse and rider. They rode a different route, which led straight off across the plain. The B ride was the intermediate and the C, which we were in, was the novice.

Last night Mom had e-mailed wishing me luck – and I needed it!

I watched Kate and Zaide set off at a good clip and vanish into the woods. Then it was our turn. Taking a long breath, I nudged Cobweb forward. A timekeeper with a clipboard made a note of the time and we set off, crossing the first field at a steady trot, Cobweb pulling furiously but controllable. We negotiated the woods where there were fallen logs to jump and low overhanging branches to watch out for. We came out by the river, at a place where an underwater causeway of flattish stones made crossing possible. And there, teetering on the muddy bank, were Kate and Zaide. Typical of Arabs, Zaide had a fear of water and had said no.

"Oh, come on!" Kate was shouting and using her legs wildly. "Come on, Zaide!"

"Want a lead?" I called.

"I wouldn't mind. We'll be here all day at this rate."

I headed Cobweb for the shallows. She splashed happily through the fast-flowing depths and Zaide, not wanting to be left behind, mustered courage and plunged in after us, high-stepping on the flat gray stones

44

and snorting at the hateful swirls of water that bubbled around her fetlocks.

We made it to the far bank. Scrambling up to the top, I threw a glance over my shoulder to see if Kate was safely across. And Cobweb, faced unexpectedly and gloriously with a wide expanse of plains, snatched at her bit and took off.

"Whoa!" I gasped, hearing Kate's frantic shouts behind me. "Cobweb, stop!"

I tried to bring her around in a circle but the reins, slippery from the splashed water, slid uselessly through my fingers.

"Steady, there!" I said over and over, but Cobweb only went all the faster.

Gray-green stretches of turf flew by in a haze and the soft thunder of racing hooves hammered in the air. There was no way I could stop. All I could do was sit tight and wait for Cobweb to tire out. To my right I glimpsed a couple of solitary riders from A group and hoped they were not Tom or Cerys. Losing control was humiliating and this first time back mattered to me. Being unable to control my horse in front of the others was a huge blow to my ego.

"Cobweb, slow down!" I gulped, clutching at a clump of mane to steady myself. "Stop, will you?"

I was starting to weaken but Cobweb felt as if she could gallop forever. On we went, hopping over tiny streamlets and bigger dykes, jumping a low barrier of gorse, tackling anything and everything that appeared in our path. I tried not to think of the rabbit holes that could bring us down, or those lethal pockets of sucking bog that could drag us under into stinking glutinous oblivion, and prayed that Cobweb was not running blind. But Cobweb was not. It struck me with a piercing suddenness that the mare knew exactly where she was heading – and there seemed all at once to be another horse there. Slightly to the rear, just out of my vision.

At first I thought it was Kate and Zaide and my heart leaped.

"Help! Kate, do something! Can't stop!"

There was no answer. Galloping on, my senses picked up the rank stink of stallion and the powerful beat of hooves that were not Zaide's.

Ahead, growing closer by the minute, was a towering mass of rock that seemed strangely familiar. Cobweb made straight for it. Reaching the foothills, she pulled at last to a lathered, heaving stop.

"Thank goodness! You silly girl! What got into you?"

Cobweb stretched her neck to draw a breath and blew gustily through flared nostrils, shaking her head with a noisy rattle of bit-rings. My hand came away sticky with sweat when I ran it soothingly across her shoulder. I threw a wary glance behind us. There was no other horse. We were completely alone.

We had arrived at one of those hilly outcrops that sometimes appear on the blank faces of barren upland. Hot and sticky from our wild flight under the blistering sun, I peered up at the needle of rock pointing to the sky and down again at its reflection in the wide, deep pool of water at our feet. It cast a dark shadow, that rock. Mountain ash, gorse and scrubby undergrowth cloaked the lower slopes of the hill in smothering swathes. No birds sang. No swarming insects jigged and buzzed. No rabbits played on the hillside or frogs swam in the pool. Apart from the slow plop of water as it seeped from fissures in the rock face, there was utter stillness and silence, and a terrible sense of sorrow and despair.

A shiver touched me and tiny spasms of fear went prickling over my skin. That was when I knew where Cobweb had brought me. It was the place in my dream. Nor was I alone as I had thought. At least, not in the usual sense. There were presences here. They were all around, crowding in on me.

Jenna, Jenna!

"No…o!" I sobbed, then louder. "No….o! Go away!"

My cry sliced the air and the voice stopped. And then, into the quiet came the unmistakable drum roll of galloping hooves. Closer, closer.

The ghost stallion! It was coming!

Chapter 4

I had to get away, and quickly. Gathering up my reins, I threw a panicked glance around. Not the plain; the hoofbeats were coming from that direction. Ahead, the rock face rose sheer and seemingly impassable out of the scrubby thickets of gorse and heather. I was penned in on all sides and Cobweb, sensing my alarm, rolled her eyes nervously.

Drum, drum, drum… the hoofbeats were closer.

Impulsively I did the only thing possible and legged Cobweb for the cover of the trees. Too late, I recalled her recent unexplained fear of woodland and she jibbed violently, pitching me from the saddle. I hit the ground with a thump that almost knocked me breathless; the reins were jerked from my grip, and through a haze of shock and pain I heard Cobweb charging off.

Those other hoofbeats were nearly here! Dragging air into my tortured lungs, I crawled underneath the bushes, hid my face in my hands and hoped for the best.

"Jenna… Jen….na!"

The voice seemed to be there again, insistent above the clamor of hooves and the breathy wheezing of the horse. There was a loud crashing in the undergrowth, a whiff of lathered horseflesh… the thud of booted feet as someone dismounted beside me. Strong hands gripped my shoulders and yanked me to my feet. Slowly the fog of pure terror cleared, and I found myself peering up into Tom's hot, puzzled face.

"Jenna, you idiot! What's the deal? Why were you hiding from me?"

He held Gold Brick by the reins. Cobweb had evidently thought the better of her bid for freedom and was hovering uncertainly behind them, her head high, nostrils quivering and reins dangling in the dust.

"The… the stallion," I stammered, fright still pounding in my veins.

"What stallion? What are you talking about? There is no stallion. Get a grip, Jenna. You lost control and got dumped and that's all there is to it." Tom broke off, glancing around. "You'd better catch Cobweb. It's no use me trying. She'll only take off and you don't want to risk losing her all over again."

His words brought me starkly to my senses. Drawing in a few more reviving breaths, I caught Cobweb, led her to a flattish boulder by the water's edge and sat down. My legs felt rubbery, my chest hurt and my shirt clung damply to my back. I brushed away a beading of sweat from my forehead and gazed dazedly up at Tom.

"Tom, what is this place?"

"Puck's Knowe? It's one of those areas of archaeological interest. There was a dig here last year. The peak is called Mani's Finger and that –" he gestured to the pool of water " – is Mani's Well. It's reputed to have magical properties. Classic, eh?" He gave his lips a comical downward quirk. "Feeling better?"

"Yes, thanks."

In fact I was feeling downright stupid. I must have looked pathetic, crouched under the bushes sniveling like a baby and letting my mare get away from me like that. The whole disastrous morning had shown me in a very bad light indeed. I was not proud of myself.

Tom was gazing at me curiously. "Come on, Jenna, spill! What really happened back there? Something must have freaked Cobweb for her to take off like that. I saw her go. You didn't have a hope of stopping her."

"Did Cerys see?" I asked in a small voice.

"I don't know. She was quite a few laps behind me. Does it matter?"

Of course it did, but I just gave a shrug. I was exhausted, defeated and fed up. And we were a long way from home.

"You'll think I've truly lost it," I said.

"Try me." Tom smiled kindly. "This isn't like you at all. There's got to be something going on."

So I told him what had happened. Tom listened, not interrupting, but letting me explain things my own way. I didn't go into details. I wanted some time to myself to mull it all over. But I touched on the midnight hoofbeats, the stallion, that compelling voice and the puzzling mark on Cobweb's neck. And, uppermost in my mind, last night's dream and the baffling way Cobweb had seemed so set on coming to this creepy place called Puck's Knowe.

"It was like she knew where she was bringing me. Tom, it was so scary. That awful silence. It's still here. Can't you feel it?"

Tom shook his head. "Can't say I do. All I can feel is the sweat running down my back. I wouldn't mind a dip in the pool."

"I wouldn't swim in there if it was the last place on earth," I said with a shudder.

"OK – but the horses might like a drink now that they've cooled off a little." Tom paused, thoughtful, then said, "I wouldn't worry too much about all this. There's usually a rational explanation for things. Cobweb's just gotten used to having her freedom. It stands to reason she'll want to run when she sees an open space like the plain. And everything else could be a simple case of reaction. You get your mare back after a stressful time, and hey! All your pent-up emotion explodes and starts to haunt you. Anybody would feel the same."

Put like that, it did make some sort of sense. Anyway, in no fit state to argue I gave a nod. "You won't tell anyone?"

"Nothing to tell," Tom said reassuringly. "Now, let's give these two a drink. Gold Brick's not into speed events. He must have wondered what was up."

I sent the cob a glance of remorse. Gold Brick stood relaxed, his nose almost touching the ground, his ears slack and eyes half-closed.

"You've both been great. Thanks, Tom."

"Oh, think nothing of it." Tom grinned. "When you're old and wrinkled you can tell your grandchildren how you were rescued by a knight in shining armor on his proud charger."

"Don't you mean sweaty sports gear and humble cob?"

"That's just the crushing sort of remark my sister would make! Speaking of Kate, we'd better make tracks. They'll be wondering about us back at the rally."

We watered the horses and started back, taking it steadily, Cobweb quiet now and subdued. By the time we reached the rally it was drawing to a close.

"Hi, you two," Kate said, riding up.

She was smiling. It turned out she had been given another attempt at the trail and now ranked among the top three contestants on points, which pleased her a lot.

"I wouldn't have left you," she went on loyally. "Except Zaide was starting to blow and I had to pull up. I saw Tom go after you so I thought I'd come back and explain what had happened."

"I don't know what's gotten into Cobweb," I grumbled. "Maybe I'm expecting too much of her too soon."

"You could be right," Kate said.

Gary Robinson, when I gave a garbled account of myself, just nodded.

"Don't worry, Jenna. You and Cobweb are both all right and that's the important thing. Better luck next time, eh?"

We were a silent trio as we headed home, each wrapped in our own thoughts.

I knew I had to accept what was happening to me. Gran would have told me to go with the flow and see where it led, that everything happens for a reason, and that it's up to me to find out what it is.

"It's no good," I blurted out, making the horses prick their ears in mild surprise. "I've got to know where Cobweb's been all this time. There are too many loose ends. Like why she's so difficult with men when she never used to be. Then there's the foal. I'd love to find it."

Kate nodded. "I don't like mysteries either. I'm as curious as you are to get to the bottom of this one. Why don't we look into it? We've got the whole vacation. What about you, Tom? Are you up for it?"

Tom did not answer right away. The horses plodded on, the clop of hooves loud in the sleepy late-afternoon stillness. Then Tom said, "I'm not sure. You got Cobweb back. Maybe it's best to leave things as they are, considering."

The last word hung between us and Kate was quick.

"Considering – what?" Her gaze went from her brother to me. "What does Tom know that I don't? It has to do with where you ended up after Cobweb bolted, doesn't it? Where *did* she go, anyway?"

"Puck's Knowe," Tom said briefly.

"Huh, she galloped a long way, then." Kate paused, sitting thoughtfully in the saddle, her long rope of hair swinging to the rhythm of Zaide's walk. "Did you know there was a dig there last summer?"

"Yes, Tom told me."

"Puck's Knowe dates back to Neolithic times, maybe earlier. The team found some symbols carved into the rock. Did you see them?"

My mouth went dry. The day had been trying enough. Freaky rock art on top of everything else was one thing too many.

"No," I said. "I didn't see anything. I wouldn't have guessed you could get up there."

"Oh, there's a path," Kate said. "You have to go around the far side of the peak to get onto it. We could ride out there sometime and I'll show you the carvings. They're really primitive. Moons and stars and animals, that sort of thing. There are horses, too. A lot of it has eroded over the centuries, but you can still make the figures out."

My hands shook on the reins and Tom flashed me a smile of concern. Kate, into her stride now, went on talking.

"The dig was great. I couldn't keep away. They opened up a burial mound but there wasn't much inside. Just the usual human remains and a few artifacts. Hammer heads, axes, you know. They had a problem dating it, so it was all kind of inconclusive in the end. Isn't that right, Tom?"

"Something like that." Tom flicked a hand over Gold Brick's mane, brushing away the flies. "I think we should give this a break."

"And I think you two should tell me what's going on," Kate countered. Her eyes narrowed to pinpoints of blue flame. "It's obvious there's something. You both look like you've swallowed vinegar. What is it? An argument?"

"Don't be silly," Tom said.

We were passing the lake. Gnats jigged on the surface and the water glittered under the hot white sun. Steam rose from the horses' flanks. My head felt cooked inside my crash helmet. I wanted a shower, a long, cold drink, and quiet.

Kate rode with her chin high and mouth set in a stubborn line. She never gave up on anything if she could help it.

Eventually the tall chimneys of Broselake came into view. We turned in at the driveway and were soon unsaddling in the cool dimness of the stable. Kate was the first to finish. She took her gear to the tack room, grabbed some cans of apple juice from the fridge in the kitchen and, handing one to Tom over Gold Brick's door, came into Cobweb's box and gave me mine.

"Oh, great. Thanks, Kate."

"No problem."

Breaking the seal, I sank down on a straw bale and drank thirstily. Then, removing my hat, I sat fluffing up my flattened hair while Kate, can in hand, went to talk to Cobweb.

"Hi, girl. You got yourself into a state with all that galloping." She put her half-empty can down on the manger, and picking up the discarded dandy brush she began raking it over Cobweb's thick and still shamefully uneven mane. "This could stand some tidying up, Jenna. Oh see, here's that mark –"

55

"Don't touch it!" I cried.

"Why not?" Kate's hand fell away. She looked at me closely. "What are you in such a funk about? It's only a brand. What's wrong with touching it?"

I wanted to say that was when I started hearing the voice and the hoofbeats, that was when I saw the gray in Cobweb's shadow. The gray that wasn't actually there.

Instead, I shrugged and said, as nonchalantly as I could, "Cobweb's twitchy, that's all. You know how she's been, freaking at things."

Kate continued to look at me with that steady blue stare. "There's more, isn't there? Are you going to tell me, or what?"

I gazed back at Kate, focusing on her coppery hair and fine-boned face. Anything rather than have to come up with an answer.

Kate was the first to glance away. "OK. So Cobweb's got a brand of some sort. At least it gives us something positive to go on. What if I ask Tom to do a search on the Internet?"

"Well, it's worth a try."

"And what if we call on the person who found Cobweb? What was her name?"

"Harriet something-or-other. Harriet … Newby, that was it. She lives in Mellbridge."

"That far? It's a long way. Still, not to worry. The roadwork will be good for the horses. When do you want to go? Tomorrow?"

"If you want," I said, warming to the idea. "Morning

might be best. Then if we get any leads we can follow up on them."

"Great." Kate threw me a determined grin. "We'll figure this out – whatever it takes. Could you do a drawing of that brand for Tom, do you think?"

Could I? I knew that mark like I knew the back of my hand!

"Not a problem," I said, getting up and reaching for Cobweb's saddle and bridle. The leather was already stiffening up and there were whitish marks on the reins where the sweat had dried. "What about the tack? Should we do it now or later? Right now I could use a shower and a some clean clothes."

"Me too. Let's do it afterwards. We could do Gold Brick's as well, and sweeten Tom up a bit. He's not exactly happy about what we're doing, is he?"

"No." I heaved a sigh. "I hate to think what Mom will say when she hears how Cobweb behaved today."

"I wouldn't tell her. Try bending the truth a little. It's what you don't say that matters."

So I told Mom when she called that Cobweb had shown what she was capable of – which was no fib. And then I mentioned Cerys Paige.

"Mom, a girl from A Group was talking about getting a new horse. I gave her our details."

"Oh. Right."

It dawned on me then that Mom seemed unusually distracted. "Mom, did you hear what I said? There's this girl who wants a horse."

57

"Mm? Oh, sorry, darling. It's been a long day. I'm a little tired. Just tell your friend – what did you say her name was?"

"I didn't. But it's Cerys Paige and she's not a friend. She's –"

"Oh, please! Not now, Jenna. Tell me some other time."

"OK. We'll talk tomorrow. 'Bye, Mom."

It wasn't until I had put my cell phone away that I realized I had not said anything about going to see Harriet Newby. But Mom clearly had other things on her mind so maybe it was just as well. I wondered what was wrong and decided she was pushing herself too hard. Dad often spoke of getting extra help on the yard, but that was as far as it went. He never had trusted anyone but us when it came to turning out a well-schooled horse.

I thought of Cerys Paige, her coldness, and her perfect clothes and flawlessly cut hair, and concluded that Cotebrook horses deserved better owners. And shrugging the matter aside, I headed off for my attic room to make the drawing for Tom.

✳ ✳ ✳

A little later, Tom took my sketch and disappeared into the lobby that Meg had made into the farm office. Knowing what Tom thought of delving into Cobweb's secret past, I did not hold out any hope that he would give the search much attention. While Tom was occupied on the office computer, I borrowed Kate's laptop and sent Gran a quick e-mail at her home on the west coast.

✳ ✳ ✳

Hi Gran,

I found a weird mark under Cobweb's mane. It's the same as a primitive symbol on a restaurant sign here. The restaurant's called the Mani. Tom told me some of the background but I don't know if there's any truth in it. At night I hear hooves and see a stallion next to Cobweb. There's this voice as well, but when I look there is never anybody there.

Gran, it's driving me crazy.
Please, can you help?
Love, Jenna.

Gran was amazing. Not only was she into waking dreams and water divining, but she was totally computer-savvy and knew just about everything from world affairs to where to get the best bargain-buys – and she could keep a secret. Dad teased her mercilessly and said if she was so gifted why couldn't she have looked into her crystal ball and found out where Cobweb had been. It was useless to tell him it didn't work that way. Dad, immeasurably practical, would only have laughed.

It was nothing for Gran to pack up on a whim and set off on her travels. She once took me on a tour of the western isles. We camped under the stars and cooked over a real campfire. Gran showed me how to call the birds from their nests and tracked down a rare orchid growing on the rocks. She said the world was full of wonder if you only opened your eyes to it.

Because she lived so far away we did not see much of Gran, but somehow I always felt close to her... and never more so than now.

As I had expected, her reply was immediate.

Hi Jenna,
How marvelous! The symbol could be a portent. You should open your mind to the voice and not be afraid.
Your Cobweb seems caught up in a tangle from the past – maybe the present, too.
Thinking of you,
Love,
Gran.

Trust Gran to talk in riddles, I thought with a sigh. Shortly afterwards, another message followed.

By the way, I have a book on primitive symbols.
Bear with me and I'll check it out.
Gran.

This time I had to smile. The walls of Gran's house were lined floor to ceiling with tattered old volumes picked up at second-hand shops and book sales. Singling one out would be no easy job. But I hadn't reckoned on Gran's extraordinary knack on being able to put her finger on exactly what she wanted. Another message came winging in.

✳ ✳ ✳

Got it!

The symbol belongs to Mani the Moon Goddess, who is said to have fulfilled her mission to mankind by driving her horse through the night skies to bring brightness, while being pursued by two terrible wolves that wanted to devour both horse and goddess, so that the world might be abandoned to everlasting dark.

Occasionally the wolves were almost successful in their chase, overtaking the chariot and all but devouring their prey. (This was said to be the reason for an eclipse.) But Mani was aided by the terrified cries of the people of the earth, which frightened the wolves off and allowed her to escape.

She'd have needed a good horse to do this night after night, wouldn't she? Could she have bred her own? Or acquired them, perhaps? I'll leave you to work that one out.
Love,
Gran.

Deleting the message, I considered what I knew so far. It was interesting that Gran's research tallied with what Tom had said. I just wished I could be more like him and Kate and see things logically and without involvement.

The strange mark, the legend of Mani, the stallion. Puck's Knowe and the rock carvings on the high peak known as Mani's Finger. There had to be a pattern here.

But how could I bring it all together? And how come I was caught up in this whole weird scenario anyway? More disturbing, what part did Cobweb play in it?

Maybe tomorrow we would come up with a few answers.

Chapter 5

We left to the sound of Tom jangling out a blues medley on his guitar, the steamy refrain growing fainter as we clopped down the rutted driveway and turned south for Mellbridge. The ride took longer than we had thought and we were both glad to see the spire of Mellbridge church rising above the trees.

Harriet Newby's slightly ramshackle but functional yard bustled with activity. Ponies were everywhere. Heads peered out of every available box and shed and a field was full to overflowing. In a pool of sunlight a little tabby cat lay washing her paws, while her four striped kittens played around her on the weedy cobblestones.

Over by a pump a girl was hosing the legs of a colt that could have been plains-bred. She directed us to a small ring, where Harriet Newby was schooling a blue-roan filly in controlled figure eights.

"Well, hi there!" Harriet cried, riding up to the gate, her round face red and smiling under the battered peak of her hat. "Cobweb's looking good. How's she been?"

"A little off, but we're getting there," I said.

Harriet Newby's gaze went with interest to Zaide, who arched her neck vainly and looked smug when she was pronounced a very nice horse indeed. "Is this purely a social call, or is there something else?" Harriet went on to inquire.

"It's about Cobweb. We wondered if you'd had any thoughts on where she'd been hiding out before you came across her."

"Well, I can only repeat what I said before." Harriet checked the filly that was trying to snatch a tuft of grass. "I bought a job-lot of youngsters at the sale and your mare was with them. This filly is one of that bunch, too. Nice little thing, isn't she?"

Harriet gave the spotted roan's neck a couple of hearty claps. Dust flew. The pony tossed its head and made another grab for the grass.

"No you don't! Sorry, but we have to learn our manners."

"Try telling Cobweb that," Kate muttered. "She attacked my brother and dumped my dad. Won't tolerate men, no way."

"Really? Was she all right before?"

"Everyone asks that," I said. "Yes, she was fine. I get the feeling no one believes me when I say how good-natured she was. Mom and Dad wouldn't have bought her otherwise. They say temperament is everything."

"I'm with them on that one," Harriet agreed. "I can give you the name of the guy who bred this little gem. There were two other ponies in the lot with his brand."

"Was it like this?

I lifted Cobweb's mane to display the mark, hoping

that Harriet would not try and touch it. Last night had been quiet. I didn't want things triggered off again.

To my relief Harriet only peered, frowning. "No, nothing like that. The one I'm talking about is a horseshoe with a hammer inside it. See?" She pointed out the brand on the filly's rump. "The breeder's grandfather was a blacksmith so I imagine it dates back to that. Come to think of it, I don't know of any like the one on Cobweb. I don't even recall noticing it on her when she was here, and I went over her very carefully. How strange. It's faint, isn't it? Not easy to make out."

"I can see it OK," I said strongly.

"Maybe it's not a real brand," Kate said, turning to Harriet. "What about the people who did the roundup? Maybe they can help?"

"I doubt it. You know how it is. They bring in masses of ponies. Nobody's likely to remember a specific animal."

"What happens afterwards?" I asked.

"Well, all the unbroken colts and fillies are sorted into lots for the sale. Each lot is numbered. As a rule, any mature animal that's been gathered up by mistake is turned out again on the plain. Cobweb must have somehow slipped through their hands. On the day I thought nothing of it. It's not unusual to get an older one thrown in with the bidding by mistake." Harriet shrugged. "There were ten in my bunch including Cobweb. It was Lot 25, if that's any help."

I bit my lip. This wasn't really getting us anywhere.

Then Harriet said, "Go and speak to the girl over

there. Ask her to print out a list of the owners of the ponies in my lot for you, and then you can speak to them personally. You never know, one of them might come up with something."

"Great," I said. "We'll let you know if we get anywhere."

"Yes, do. I'd be interested."

She sent us a salute and returned to her schooling, the filly's small hooves stirring up clouds of dust that tickled my nostrils and brought on a sudden sneezing attack.

We came away with not only the names and addresses of the owners, but their respective brand markings too. Other than that, we weren't much better off.

"And I really thought we'd get a few leads," Kate said as we headed home disappointed.

"It's a little bit of a letdown, isn't it? At least we've got names to follow up. There were four different owners in Lot 25. They're all spread out over a pretty wide area."

"Getting around to them all will take forever. Why don't we split up and each make a call? Tom too. It'll save time."

"That is if Tom can be persuaded," I said doubtfully.

"He'd better. Come on, let's get back and ask him…"

When we arrived at Broselake, Tom was rubbing down Gold Brick on the yard. And with him was Cerys.

"You've been gone a long time," Tom called out. He put down the stable rubber and rested his elbows on the cob's back. "Any luck?"

"Not really," I said.

Cerys went to pat Zaide. "Hi, pony. Goodness, you do feel hot. Hello, Kate."

66

"Hi." Kate's lips snapped together. She hated Zaide being called a pony. Arabs were always referred to as horses and Zaide was well up in size.

Cerys turned her attention to Cobweb. She had taken off her hard hat and her hair perfectly framed the smooth oval of her face. Even in the sweltering midday heat she appeared fresh and totally together.

"Hello, Cobweb. Aren't you cute?" Cerys purred. "I had a pony like this once. I must have been about ten or eleven. I don't remember its name but it was a fantastic jumper."

"Is that right?" I replied coolly.

Merridance was gazing out over the door of Zaide's box, which Kate had mucked out in preparation for our return, and her lips tightened even more.

"I think Kate wants to put Zaide in, Cerys," Tom said. "Could you tie Merridance up on the yard for now?"

"No need. I was just going."

Taking her time, fully aware of everyone's eyes on her, Cerys collected her hat from the gatepost where she had left it and went to fetch her horse. "I'm afraid the box will need some attention – sorry about that," she said, mounting. She looked at Tom. "It's been great. See you tomorrow? Same time?"

"Yeah, OK. Here, let me open the gate."

Tom went over to the big wooden stock-gate, which his dad insisted on keeping closed at all, times, and Cerys went trotting away without a backward glance. Closing the gate with a clang, Tom grabbed a stable-basket and rubber gloves and gave the box a quick cleaning, throwing down more straw. Then, indicating to Kate that all was as she had left it, he gestured her and Zaide in with a dramatic flourish of his hand and went back to grooming his horse.

"I could strangle that girl, I really could," Kate muttered.

"She certainly knows how to wind people up," I said, dismounting stiffly.

Tom reappeared as we were hanging up our gear in the tack room. "Tell me what happened this morning."

"Not a lot," Kate said. "We got the names of the owners in the job-lot of ponies that Cobweb turned up in, and that's about it."

"What about the horse and moon brand?"

"Harriet Newby had never seen it before," I said.

"That's no surprise." Tom gave a shrug. "There's no such brand recorded with the Mountain and Plains Society. I did come across something else you might find interesting, though. Cobweb wasn't the only horse to go missing the way she did. There have been twelve other reported cases over the past five years. They were all nicely bred animals. Each one vanished and turned up again after a space of time. Just like Cobweb."

"Wow! Did any of them have the brand?"

"There was no mention of it. None was a local case. They were all spread out over a big area."

"Were they all mares?" Kate asked thoughtfully.

"Now that you mention it, yes, they were," Tom said.

"I wonder if any of them had had a foal," I said.

"The report didn't give that much detail. It just said they reappeared some eighteen to twenty months after disappearing. I daresay there could have been others. Not everyone reports a missing animal and ponies and other livestock have always run off and survived perfectly well on the plain."

"But these were quality mares. You'd have thought the owners would have looked into it more seriously," Kate said.

"I think the general conclusion was that they had escaped their yards and lived rough with the wild herds. Like I said, that's always happened around here." Tom was studying the list from Harriet Newby's yard. "Are you following up on this?"

"Yes, I think so," I said.

"Two of those addresses are pretty close to home," Kate said. "They're both female owners so it might be best if Jenna does those. If I do the guy on East Ridge, Tom, could you do the one on Western Point?"

"Oh... if you like," Tom said, without enthusiasm. "When were you thinking of going?"

"Tomorrow?" I said.

"Tomorrow's out. I promised Cerys we'd go for a trail ride."

Kate made a face. "She's pathetic!"

"Cerys is all right," Tom said. "She's in my year at school. She's very popular."

"Yeah, with the boys," Kate said in disgust, and Tom grinned.

"The teachers like her fine. She plays clarinet in the school orchestra and she can sing too. She's got a terrific voice for jazz. She brought the roof down at a charity show we gave in the spring. I backed her on the guitar. It was great."

I swallowed hard. Straight singing and folk I could manage. Jazz was beyond my scope – and I knew if I practiced every day for the next hundred years I could never, ever master an instrument as technically challenging as the clarinet. Tom could say what he liked about music being all down to attitude. I knew my limitations.

Up until now I had never thought of Tom as a boyfriend. He had always been, well… Tom. It had taken someone like Cerys to make me see him differently. I had the uncomfortable feeling that the dislike I felt for her stemmed from a bad case of jealousy.

"Well, I'm going tomorrow," I said.

"So am I," Kate added.

"OK." Tom grimaced. "I still think you should leave it alone, but if you insist on going ahead with this crazy scheme I suppose it's best to get that side of things taken care of. We can do Western Point instead of where we'd planned. You'd better tell me what kind of questions I should ask this guy, Jenna."

"Oh, you know. If he remembers seeing Cobweb at all. Which herd she was with. That sort of thing."

"I'm with you. What about this brand you've been talking about. Let's have a look at it."

We went back to the stables and Tom took the

precaution of staying by the door of the box to avoid another fit of tantrums. With Kate at Cobweb's head, I pushed back the mane to reveal what lay beneath.

"It's not very clear," Kate said, squinting at the mark that I could see quite distinctly.

Tom shrugged. "It doesn't look like anything much to me."

"Harriet Newby made it out this morning," I said, indignant. "You did yourself, Kate."

"Well… yes." Kate sounded doubtful. "It must be wearing off."

"A brand wouldn't," Tom said matter-of-factly. "Once it's been done it's there for life. It must be something else."

"Cobweb had that patchy scurf, didn't she?" Kate said. "It could be that and you mistook it for a pattern, Jenna. It's easily done."

"It's a moon and horse," I choked, thinking I really was losing it. Why was it that I could see the symbol and they couldn't? "The restaurant at Ravensmoor has the same pattern around the edge of the signboard."

"There you are, then." Kate looked triumphant. "You saw that and thought the blotch on Cobweb's neck resembled it. Mystery solved."

"But Harriet saw it!" I argued. "She said it was hard to make out but she definitely understood what it was. She said she'd never seen a brand like it."

"Maybe she was being tactful," Kate said.

"Oh, let's leave it," Tom cut in. "I'm going to call Cerys about the change of plan."

He sent us a slightly exasperated glance and left.

"I don't envy him," Kate said. "Cerys is the pits when things don't go her way. Serves Tom right. He should be more choosy who he rides with."

She sniffed dismissively and said she'd better check out our routes for the next day.

When she had gone I turned back to Cobweb and, taking a deep breath, I tentatively touched the symbol on her neck. As before, the icy pangs shot through me. I heard a rushing, rustling sound, and in the darkest corner of the box a figure appeared. Her long robes and flowing hair wreathed about her. She gazed straight at me and raised her hand, beckoning.

"No," I whispered, rigid with fright. "Go away."

The figure vanished. And almost at once another image appeared. It was a ragged line of trees on what seemed like the edge of the high plain, but even as I gazed the picture fractured and faded away, and I was left standing in the box, white and shaken. Cobweb, totally oblivious, turned her head and nudged me hard in the chest, and then from the house Kate called, saying she had mapped out the routes for tomorrow, and was I coming to check them with her?

Chapter 6

The first address I went to the next morning was a white-painted cottage with stabling and big grassy paddocks. The woman there shook her head apologetically.

"Sorry, but I can't help you. My ponies get scattered all over the place. It's hard to keep track of them all."

"Are you sure you haven't seen Cobweb before?"

"Oh, quite sure," the woman said. "I wouldn't have forgotten. She's not plains-bred, is she? If I'd come across her I'd have reported it to the Patrol. She's far too well-bred looking to be running loose with the herds."

I asked a few more questions, but none of the answers were what I needed so I thanked the woman and rode away.

I wondered if Kate was having more luck. Or Tom. Was he even paying much attention to what he was doing, jogging along with Cerys in the sunshine? I thought of them, Cerys hanging on Tom's words as if he were the only one in the world for her, and I was not very happy when I arrived at the second house on my route.

A barrage of barking met us from a row of kennels at the back of the house, and Cobweb snorted warily. The resident was a harassed-looking woman with three small children. She was holding on to the collar of a glossy black Labrador whose rumbling growls, together with the noise of the other dogs and constant interruption from the little girls, did not make conversation easy.

"Have I seen your mare before, did you say? Oh, be quiet, Murphy!" The woman spoke sternly to the dog, while trying to look Cobweb over. "No, I don't think so."

Through the open doorway of a wooden shed I could see a notice board covered with rosettes she must have won with the dogs and the ponies at shows.

"I'm trying to find out where Cobweb could have been. She had a mark like a brand on her neck," I went on hastily. "A horse inside a crescent-moon?"

I was saved from the embarrassment of showing her the symbol that others did not seem able to make out by the kennel dogs, who were still making such a din that the woman went to quiet them. She was soon back, the black one in tow.

"Sorry about that. You were saying?"

"We think Cobweb may have been living wild on the plain. She would have been shaggier than she is now. Mom and Dad had a tough time recognizing her when we got her back."

"They do grow heavy coats, don't they?" The woman smiled and looked suddenly quite pretty. "No, I'm sure I'd know this one. She's very nice. Sorry, haven't been much help, have I?"

"Well, thanks all the same."

I was about to leave when she stopped me.

"One moment. That mark you mentioned – the horse and crescent moon? I've just remembered something. My husband is an archaeologist. He's away working at the moment, which is why I haven't been able to get around to the herds as much as I would like. Well, I'm a bit tied up here, what with the children and everything."

She paused to attend to the smallest girl who had tumbled over on her fat little backside and was bawling lustily. "There, Rosy. You're not hurt. Go and find Tania. Tell her to get you a cookie."

The crying stopped instantly. The little girl waddled off.

"Now, where was I? Oh, I remember. Are you familiar with a place called Puck's Knowe? My husband headed the team there when it was excavated. One of the artifacts they found had a symbol carved onto it that sounds like what you described."

"Are you certain?" I said, heart skipping a beat.

"Oh, yes. It's all coming back to me. It was carved on a fragment of rock. My husband called it the Seal of Mani."

Wow!

I thought of the rock carvings Kate had mentioned. *Stars and moons and animals*. Was there a horse and crescent-moon as well? There was one way to find out.

"There weren't all that many artifacts," the woman went on. "But that's often the case with very early excavations of this kind. You could see what turned up if you're interested. It's all on display at the museum in Buxton."

"Thanks, I might do that," I said breathlessly, and gathered up my reins.

Riding away, I had not realized that the dog had gained his freedom until he came pounding up behind us and I reined in sharply, expecting trouble. But Cobweb only danced about a bit and the Labrador thought the better of it and went galloping off back to the house.

"Good girl," I said, patting her.

She had to be improving. She hadn't over-reacted when the dogs had barked, nor, I remembered, had she shied at Tom yesterday in the stable. Asking her to trot, we headed off to Broselake in a far happier frame of mind.

Kate was already there when I clattered into the farmyard. She was putting Zaide in the paddock and waved from the gate. Soon afterwards Tom came clopping in on Gold Brick.

"Waste of time," he said, jumping down and running the stirrups up the leathers. "The guy was out when we got there so we had to hang around for a while." To judge from Tom's expression this had not suited Cerys one bit. "We were about to give up and come home when he turned up. He'd been doing the rounds of the herds."

"Did he know anything about Cobweb?"

"I described her as well as I could but he couldn't recall having seen anything like her. He seemed a bit stressed out, actually. There'd been some trouble on his side of the plain. That's why he'd been checking his ponies."

"What sort of trouble?" Kate asked.

"I don't know. He didn't go into details. He wanted to make some phone calls so we left. That's about it, really."

"I didn't get anywhere, either," Kate said. "What about you, Jenna?"

For some reason I was reluctant to say what I had discovered. It wasn't much to go on and until I had more information there seemed little point. Kate would only have been dismissive and Tom obviously had other things on his mind.

So I shrugged and said neither of the owners had recognized Cobweb, and left it at that.

"You're a puzzle," I said to Cobweb as I rubbed her down. "Are you missing your foal? Poor girl. I wish we could find it for you."

She put her nose in my palm and heaved a huge sigh, as if she wished it too.

✳ ✳ ✳

The next morning Kate said she wanted to put Zaide through some track work, so I grabbed the opportunity to follow up on my lead. There was some shopping I needed to do as well, and leaving Kate frowning over a dressage test from the saddle, I ran and caught the bus into Buxton. It turned out that the museum did not open until noon and to pass the time I went into the public library, where a heritage exhibition was being held.

And there, on one of the displays, was the story of Mani the Moon.

Some local schoolchildren had made a collage of

her journey across the night sky. She rode in a silver-foil chariot drawn by a single milk-white horse, which had bulging muscles and snorting nostrils and looked powerful and strong.

Below, in a moonlit meadow, was a herd of mares and foals.

The moon horses.

The children had written out the legend in their careful print, which I read with interest. The moon horses were said to have gathered up the earthly mares as they traveled across the skies in order to boost their stock.

Maybe the moon horses took her.

Into my mind leapt the words of the elderly villager back home. I gulped, turning my attention back to the figures. Drawn with such childlike simplicity and lack of any real skill, they closely resembled the symbol on Cobweb's neck, which burned so brightly in my memory. The two wolves had been drawn in sharp relief, paying great attention to their hungry eyes, pointed fangs and long, dripping tongues.

"I wouldn't like to meet those two in the dark, would you?" said a woman at my side. She had a lively face and intelligent dark eyes.

"Not really," I said. "The moon horses must have been scary as well. People used to threaten their children with them when they were naughty."

"Really? I haven't heard that one before. But then these stories get distorted over the years, don't they? I'd have thought the wolves indicated a bad force and the horses just the opposite. Though I suppose it's a question for debate. You'd have to ask Mani herself to get to the truth."

She moved off, laughing, and leaving me with the uneasy thought that her light-hearted remark could be a lot more plausible than she knew.

The hands of the clock over the entrance pointed to almost twelve, and I left the building and went on to the museum, arriving as the doors were opening.

Tucked away in a corner of the main gallery was what I had come to see – a small assembly of fragments from the dark and misty past. Flints, arrowheads, pieces of rock-hard wood that may once have been the prop of an ancient straw-thatched roundhouse all met my gaze. And bones – human and animal. There were also some beautifully crafted cloak-clasps and other adornments wrought in silver and gold.

In a separate cabinet was what I most wanted to see – a broken section of flat stone with a carving of a chunky little horse inside a thin wedge of a new moon.

I caught my breath. It was the exact replica of the one I knew.

Even as I stared at it, that strange, harsh whispering started up again in my head.

Jenna, Jenna…

"Oh, *please!*" I swallowed, knuckles clenching whitely. "Go away, can't you?"

My voice echoed in the silent confines of the building and the curator at his desk looked up with a frown. The whispering was still there, an incomprehensible jumble, and suddenly I had to get out, away from the past and its mysteries. Dragging my gaze from the symbol, I retraced my steps along the gallery and went out into the sunshine.

In the street all was reassuringly normal. Shoppers and vacationers strolled past, laughing and talking, and a stream of traffic waited for the lights to change. The voice had stopped. Taking out my shopping list, I headed off for the gift store on the corner.

Here I bought Mom two large bars of her favorite Buxton chocolate, a giant slab of the local toffee that Dad couldn't get enough of, and stocked up on mints for Cobweb. Gran collected fridge magnets, so I chose one of a prancing pony to send her and picked up a paperback Meg had said she wanted.

I was about to leave the shop when a display of postcards showing local scenes caught my attention. And there, staring me in the face, was the symbol I had just fled from. Another postcard showed the signboard on the Mani restaurant in Ravensmoor.

I wanted yet again to escape, but then I remembered what Gran had said.

Open your mind to the voice and don't be scared.

So steeling myself, I compromised and purchased the two postcards before hurrying off to catchd my bus. All the way back as we rumbled along narrow country lanes, chugging up the hills and sailing down the other sides, the voice nudged on the edges of my mind. I wondered if the moon goddess was trying to tell me something crucial, and shied away from the thought. I hated the freaky symbol on my mare's neck and the strange vibes it gave off. No way was I going to touch it again.

At Broselake, Kate was waiting for me by Cobweb's box. Excitement glowed on her face.

"Jenna, take a look at this!"

She pushed a copy of the local newspaper at me, jabbing a finger at a column at the bottom of the page.

There was a caption.

IS THIS A RETURN OF MANI THE MENACE?

The article was a humorous media report on a serious subject – serious to horse and pony owners, that is. Sightings had been logged of a rider in long robes galloping across the plain at night. People were being frightened off from visiting their favorite spots. The report made a comment about the likelihood of the old gods returning to haunt and ended with a list of places where the figure had been seen.

Last on the list was Mellbridge.

"That's where Harriet Newby lives."

"Exactly," Kate said. "And some of the other places tally with the list Tom got off the Internet. You know, where the mares had gone missing?"

"How strange."

"Isn't it? And that's not all. Not long after you'd gone Mom said she needed some bread so I rode to the village to get some. The shop was buzzing. A farmer from the other side of Ravensmoor was bringing in his sheep when this apparition appeared out of nowhere. It was getting dark and difficult to see but it sounded like the one in the article. The farmer's two dogs were so freaked out they ran off. One of them arrived back home later, but the other one is still missing. It's the mother of his best trials dog. He's really miserable about it."

"I bet. Was he on foot?"

"No, he was riding a pony that sounded like Dad's old Magpie. It went crazy and all the sheep scattered. It made me think of those hoofbeats you mentioned, Jenna."

I opened my mouth to speak and shut it again. I still wasn't sure how Kate would react if I told her all I knew.

Kate's eyes narrowed. "You know something, don't you? Tom does, too. I'm not a complete idiot, Jenna. I wish you'd let me in on it."

"Well…"

I bit my lip, then decided to go for it. Beckoning Kate into the box where we were less likely to be overheard, I told her more or less what I had said to Tom. Some of it, the really confusing parts, I kept back. There were parts to this equation that applied only to people like Gran and myself. The voice, the vibes when I touched the mark on Cobweb's crest, the shadowy images in the stable and the bone-chilling experience at Puck's Knowe… all this I made light of.

Lastly, I told her where I had been that day.

Kate listened, sitting on the manger, one leg swinging, her sharp blue gaze fixed on my face. When I came to a stop there was a thoughtful silence, into which came the sound of Cobweb munching at the hayrack.

"Well…" Kate gave a little shrug. "I don't know what to say, really. Some people are supposed to be doomed so I guess you must be one of them."

"I didn't think you'd believe it. Even to me it sounds far-fetched. Moon horses! It'll be wolves next."

"Oh, didn't I tell you?" Kate said in a voice that was only a shadow of its usual self. "That's what all the panic was at the shop. Someone who lives on the plain was woken in the night by howling."

"It could have been a dog."

"That's what I said. This person was certain it wasn't. It turned out she'd been on a wolf trail somewhere so she knew the difference."

"Ugh!" I drew a shuddery breath.

All at once Kate became typically, efficiently, herself. Sliding down from the manger, she threw back Cobweb's mane and peered at the crest of her neck.

"All I can see is a sort of smudge, like a scar. But you seem to see it differently. It's weird. But then a lot of this is weird." She came to the door where I stood, the newspaper in my hand. "Jenna, I haven't got a clue what this is all about, but it's always best to face things head on. If you say you heard galloping and all the rest of it, I'll have to take your word for it. The dream was something else. To dream of a place you never even knew existed, and then be bolted off with to the very spot? That's mind-blowing. Why don't we ride over to Puck's Knowe and investigate? I could show you where the rock carvings are."

"What – now?"

"Any reason why not?"

A shiver ran down my spine. I could think of a dozen reasons for avoiding Puck's Knowe and began stammering them out. It was a long way. What if we got caught out in the dark? Anyway, I hadn't had anything to eat and I was starving.

"So am I," Kate said. "We could grab a sandwich first. We'll take the dogs with us. Stop making excuses, Jenna. We'll be fine."

Out on the yard, the sun still shone brightly although it was low in the sky. I could hear Tom arguing with his dad as they sorted out some ewes for market the next day. It all felt wonderfully ordinary and safe. No way did I want to visit that spooky rock and dark pool. On the other hand, I was curious to see the carvings... and Cobweb had not yet been out and needed the exercise.

Kate was already opening the loosebox door.

"I'm going to saddle Zaide. If we go now we can easily get there and back before dark."

She paused, daring me to refuse.

"OK, let's go," I said.

Chapter 7

We set off at a brisk trot, clattering past the lake, through the avenue of trees and over the bridge, Jess and Taggle bounding along at the horses' heels. Ravensmoor drowsed in the late-afternoon sunshine. At the forge, all was quiet. Crossing the next bridge, we entered the first fringes of the plain.

Everything shimmered under the great expanse of sky. Sheep lay dozing in the bracken with their half-grown lambs. In the lazy summer heat, even the birds were quiet.

"Let's canter," Kate said, shortening her reins.

We shot off along the trail, hooves thudding dully on the hard ground, the dogs streaking alongside. Ahead, the high peak of Puck's Knowe grew ever closer and Cobweb, realizing where we were going, became suddenly skittish.

"Behave," I said, checking her.

"Oh, leave her alone." Kate threw me a grin, bouncing along, Zaide's coat glinting gold in the sunlight. "I've been reading about natural horsemanship. It's the very opposite of conventional riding but it makes sense. If a horse or pony wants to gallop you don't argue. Let's have a race. Jess! Taggle! Come on!"

She leaned forward in the saddle and Zaide quickened her pace. Cobweb did the same, traveling not at the wild bolt of last time but a controlled gallop that gobbled up the ground in pounding strides. We powered on, the dogs shooting ahead, scenting water and a cooling drink.

Cobweb was the first to reach the outcrop. We pulled up, dancing as Zaide came hurtling in with Kate laughing so much she could hardly use her reins.

"Wow, that was great! Where have those dogs gone?"

"They're over there by that clump of gorse," I answered her.

The collies had slaked their thirst at the pool and flopped down in the shade, heads up, tongues lolling. Their gaze was fixed on the jagged point of Mani's Finger, and at once all my elation faded. Around me, Puck's Knowe was exactly the same as before; silent, watchful... waiting.

I gave a little involuntary shudder, and Kate saw.

"Jenna, you can't be *cold*! It's absolutely sweltering!" She waved a hand in the vague direction of the rock. "The path is over there. We can ride part of the way up but after that it gets steeper. We'll have to lead the horses then. Walk on, Zaide."

Narrow, stony, and barely discernable from below, the path wound a treacherous route around the peak, going steeply upwards. As we went I wondered what other feet had trod this way centuries ago when the world was a younger place and people worshipped the old gods.

Up and up we went, the horses' hooves kicking up tiny

pebbles and loose shale. About halfway up we dismounted and led them, the sheer bulk of the rock face to our left and on the right, a drop to the tree-covered ground below. The dogs still lay in the same spot, two black and white dots against the flare of yellow gorse. The sheep were like scattered drifts of snow across the gray-green face of the plain. Over in the west, the sun was beginning to set.

Kate stopped abruptly, pointing. "There it is."

Sure enough, carved into the ridged gray surface of the rock was a series of ancient symbols. Time and weather had done their worst, nibbling and erasing, but the drawings could still be seen.

I took in the moon in her various sequences, the stars in formation, the glorious sunburst. Shapes of animals went dancing across the rock face – deer, cattle, the fierce little swine of the forest with their sharply curving tusks and quick eyes.

Intrigued, I looked further.

"Here it is. The moon and horse. The breeder I was talking to yesterday told me her husband called it the Seal of Mani. He was an archaeologist. He'd worked on the excavations here."

"Really? You never said that." Kate was pulling away tufts of grass and tiny harebells that grew from fissures in the rock. "Here's another one. And another. It makes a pattern. I wonder what it means?"

At that moment there was a high-pitched keening sound from below. The horses' ears shot up. I felt the hairs rise on the nape of my neck.

"What's going on?" Kate said, peering over the edge.

Jess was sitting bolt upright, her head thrown back, howling. After a moment Taggle joined in and their singing flowed in waves toward the point of the rock above us. The sound was having a peculiar effect on me. I was aware of a sinking sensation, as if the present was falling away and the past reasserting itself. Before my eyes, everything began to waver and change. The plain itself was much the same but the crimson-setting sun had gone and a cold distinct wind blew, smelling of snow. Voices carried, a sort of chanting... and then that other voice started up, a dark mantra in my head.

"What a din!" Kate muttered. Looping the Arab's reins over her arm, she cupped her hands to her mouth and hollered to the dogs, "Hey, you two! Cut it out! Quiet!"

The collies, usually so obedient, took not one bit of notice.

"What's the matter with them?" Kate frowned angrily. "We'd better go and see. You go first, Jenna."

I could see her lips moving and hear her voice, but that other voice was crowding out what Kate was saying and all I could do was gaze at her mutely, caught between one world and another. Kate faltered, staring. Then she seized my arms and shook me hard.

Instantly, the present refocused itself.

"Jenna! You went all weird on me. What happened?"

I swallowed hard, still tasting the snow of that long-gone winter. "It's... it's this place. I told you. It's freaky."

By now Zaide was thoroughly spooked and started

to back up nervously on the narrow path. Her hooves dislodged a few small stones that went tumbling over the edge and bouncing over the jutting boulders all the way down to the bottom. Cobweb seemed more excited than scared and kept gazing about her, as if she expected something to happen.

"Walk on, girl," I said as firmly as I could.

We began the steep descent, concentrating on keeping our feet on the slippery path. At some point the dogs stopped howling. Arriving at the small plateau, we mounted up and rode the rest of the way down.

Jess and Taggle greeted us with troubled whines and faintly quivering tails.

"What was all the noise about?" Kate asked them, dismounting.

In response the dogs ran off a short way and stood, staring ahead and whimpering a little. The sun had now set and the plain was taking on the shadowed bleakness of approaching dusk. Above us, Mani's Finger gleamed dully in the afterglow. But it wasn't at this that the dogs were now fixing their gaze, but a mound of earth-packed boulders not far from the pool.

"That's the burial place I told you about," Kate said.

Prickly gorse and clumps of purpling heather grew thickly at its base, disguising the fact that this might be anything but a natural part of the landscape.

Jess gave another more urgent whine.

"It's like she's trying to tell us something." I strained my ears. "Listen! Can you hear anything?"

Faintly, from the direction of the mound, came the low, moaning wail of an animal in distress. Both reaching the same conclusion at once, we exchanged a glance.

"It's got to be the lost sheepdog," Kate said. "Goodness knows how it got in there. The chamber was blocked off after the dig for safety reasons."

"They couldn't have done a very good job. Poor thing. It must have gone in there to hide and got trapped."

"We'd better take a look," Kate said.

"But…" I was hesitant. "Should we?"

"Of course. Oh, come on, Jenna. There's nothing in there any more. The poor dog may be hurt."

That settled it.

Tethering the horses with the baling twine we always carried for this purpose, we began to move aside some of the smaller boulders from around the entrance. The earth was surprisingly loose and it did not take long to enlarge the narrow cleft in the rock that the dog must have squeezed through. Once the hole was big enough, we peered in. Utter blackness met us, but glimmering red in the inky dark of the cavern beyond, a pair of eyes watched us balefully.

Jess and Taggle began to dig, sandy soil and tiny stones flying out in all directions, and after a while we were able to remove a larger rock, giving us better access. Kneeling, we tried to coax the animal out.

"Come on, girl." Kate clicked her fingers encouragingly. "Good girl. Come on."

The eyes blinked, but came no closer. At our side

Jess and Taggle whimpered anxiously. We called and whistled, all to no avail.

"This is hopeless," I said at last. Sitting back on my heels, I looked around. Dusk was thickening rapidly. A cloud of bats swooped overhead with a chorus of shrill squeaks. The first stars had appeared in the west. "Kate, if we stick around here much longer we're going to hit the dark on the way back."

Kate bit her lip. Neither of us had thought to bring our cell phone with us. All we could do now was go home and give the alert. But the thought of leaving the dog all alone and perhaps injured was unbearable.

"We're not going anywhere till we get her out," Kate said stoutly.

We redoubled our efforts, the blue dusk gathering inexorably around us.

"She must be thirsty," Kate said. "Could you get some water from the pool? Here, you can use my hat to put it in. It may entice her out."

Hurriedly I did as she asked and little by little, drawn by the tantalizing prospect of a drink after many hours without, the sheepdog bellied her way toward our outstretched hands.

"Got her!" I gasped.

Grasping the dog by the scruff of her neck, we eased her, blinking and scrabbling, through the aperture to freedom. Once out, she shook herself and glanced nervously around her. She was a mottled gray with the rangy look of a working animal, and seemed more frightened and exhausted than hurt.

Kate offered the water. The sheepdog made a first few tentative laps, then finished off the rest gratefully. Jess and Taggle, after greeting the runaway with playful waves of their tails, sat down to wait and see what happened next.

Getting the stray home was a problem. She was too wobbly to make it under her own steam, besides which we didn't want to risk losing her all over again. Then Kate suggested putting her across Zaide's saddle.

"I'll make a harness with the baling twine. It'll give me something to hang on to, isn't that right, girl?"

She fondled the dog and it licked her hand as if in agreement.

Kate was attaching the homemade harness when I happened to notice something on the floor of the chamber. Delving inside, I pulled out a shabby canvas head collar and a length of rope.

"What's this doing in there?"

"No clue. Someone must have been messing around in there. I thought the stones seemed loose by the entrance."

"Ugh. I can't think who'd want to."

"Oh, I don't know. Kids from the riding school go on picnic rides to Puck's Knowe. Mucking around in an old tomb would be just their thing. They'd shove the stones back in case they got found out." Kate tied the final knot in the twine. "There. We'd better hurry. Shove that gear back inside and let's block the hole up again."

Once Kate was in the saddle with the sheepdog in front, I mounted Cobweb and we set off, Kate grumbling because her hat was uncomfortably soggy.

The journey back seemed to take forever. With Kate holding grimly on to the runaway, we rode at a sober walk and watched the long fingers of darkness come stealing across the plain. Jess and Taggle knew their way and were aware, with that uncanny instinct that dogs have, that we depended on them to keep us clear of the danger spots like bogs and dykes. The sheepdog, weakened and trusting, lay quietly across the pommel of the saddle, anticipating home and her dinner.

"That's going to be one happy owner," I said into the quiet.

"Definitely." Kate shifted her position in the saddle, easing first one aching arm, then the other. "Phew, I'll be glad to get back."

The farm where the rally was held came into view, then the village where the street lamps cast an orange beam, and at last we were clattering up the rutted driveway to Broselake.

Tom must have been watching out for us and came to open the gate.

"We were getting anxious," he said. "Did you get lost, or what?"

"Long story," Kate replied. "Don't just stand there, Tom. Lift this dog down and make sure she doesn't get away from you. Jenna, could you do Zaide for me, please? I'm going to find Dad. He'll know how to get in touch with the owner."

✳ ✳ ✳

Much later, one overjoyed farmer reunited with his dog and gone with Daniel to the Mani to celebrate, the three of us sat in the office and talked over the events of the day. Tom laughed when we mentioned the find in the burial chamber.

"Head collar and lead rope? It had to be kids."

"I can think of better places to hang about," I said. "Puck's Knowe gives me the creeps. Jess and Taggle didn't think much of it either. Wow, what a racket!"

"That was because of the dog," Kate said.

"I'm talking about before. They were looking up at the peak."

"Oh, Jenna! That's your imagination getting the better of you. There's nothing wrong with Puck's Knowe. The dig was great. You'd have loved it."

"I wouldn't. I hate it when people's remains are dug up and carted off to be carbon-dated and all that."

"Why? It's only a load of old bones."

"But they've been put to rest. It's disturbing them."

"Mm, I can see where you're going but if they didn't investigate we'd never find out about the past. I think archaeology has a lot going for it."

"Then maybe that's what you should look at for a career, Kate," Tom said.

He paused, then held up the newspaper with the article on the "haunting." "What do you two think of this? Who'd be crazy enough to dress up in fancy robes and gallop around on the plain at night?"

"People do crazy things," Kate said dismissively. "It's got to have something to do with the horse Jenna heard that time. So much for spooky theories."

I thought of the stubby gray stallion, the sort that would have roamed the high plains when Puck's Knowe and the area all around would have been home to communities of warring clans, and tried to recall if there had been a rider on those midnight sightings. It was impossible. The image was too blurred. All I could conjure up was an outline of the horse, the persistency of the voice and the menacing thunder of hooves.

A silence had fallen, into which came the shrill ringing of the telephone on the desk. Before any of us could answer it Meg had picked up the extension in the kitchen.

"Jenna?" she called out. "It's your Mom. You can take it in here if you like. I'm going to take a shower."

"Coming." I went through and picked up the telephone. "Hi, Mom. How are things?"

"Oh, all right… I suppose."

My stomach lurched. Mom was the true optimist. Nothing ever got her down. This wasn't the response I expected.

"Mom, what's happened? Is it Dad?"

"Oh, no, nothing like that, " Mom said hastily. "We're both fine. It's… well, you know that filly we had in for schooling?"

"The two-year-old?"

"Yes. Last night the owner called saying he'd changed his mind and was sending the horse to another yard. He came to get her himself this morning."

"But… did he say why?"

"Not exactly. Only that he'd heard bad reports of Cotebrook."

"You're joking!"

"I only wish I was," Mom said sadly.

I was incredulous. Carter Harrison, the filly's owner, was notoriously hard to please but so far there had been no grumbles with what we had turned out for him.

"Mom, this is crazy. Our yard has a terrific reputation."

"Unblemished to date," Mom said. "Dad and I have gone over it until we're sick of the subject. Neither of us can come up with a reason. Dad thinks Carter Harrison may be getting us mixed up with another yard but I can't see it, myself. Whatever, mud sticks. We had two more youngsters booked in for next month and this afternoon the owner called and cancelled. She wouldn't say why, and this is an established customer. We must have trained dozens of horses for her."

"Mom, this is awful. It's got to be a mistake. Isn't there anything you can do?"

"Not without finding out how the rumors started, and that's no easy matter." Mom drew a furious breath. "These gossip-mongers are all the same. One sniff of trouble and they have a field day and before you know it you have an empty stable."

"But there hasn't been any trouble," I protested.

"N...no. Someone Dad knows hinted that it could be connected with Cobweb's disappearance. It's been suggested we manufactured it so we could claim on the insurance.

Admittedly, funds were short at the time, but it was nothing desperate and certainly innocent enough. We were simply being careful with our finances so we could go ahead with the new indoor ring we'd been planning. I suppose it may have looked a little suspicious to an outsider."

"Why should it? Everyone cuts back on spending at some point."

There were no secrets at our house. I knew all about the highs and lows of running a business. And Mom and Dad had always talked freely of their hopes and plans. Nothing as shady as cooking up an insurance scam had ever entered the conversation and never would. I also knew how swiftly a thriving concern could take a dip for the worse. Any more cancellations, and Cotebrook would no longer score in the top league of training establishments, where it had been for several years now.

The complexities of insurance were beyond me but I tried to think this through. "Did Dad make a claim for Cobweb?" I asked.

"No, he didn't. That's what has gotten to me more than anything. We always hoped we'd be able to trace her – it wasn't for want of trying. If the worst had happened and we could have proved she'd gone for the meat trade or whatever, there would have been a sound reason for claiming. As it was, everything was so uncertain. So Dad kept the policy open. Do you see?"

"Yes, I think so."

"Some nasty minded individual has been spreading the poison. If I could get my hands on whoever it is…"

Mom's voice took on a steely note. She seemed about to say more, but then she gave a little sigh and went on to ask about Cobweb and if I was enjoying the vacation. After what I had just heard I was reluctant to go into details, so I just told her that Cobweb was getting better every day, which was true.

"You and Kate were talking about a camping ride," Mom said. "Have you had any more thoughts about it?"

"Not really. I wanted to see how Cobweb shaped up. I suppose we could go ahead."

"Well, I wouldn't leave it too long. This fine weather won't last forever and it's not much fun camping in the rain. Remember doing the coast with Gran? She said afterwards it rained so much she was afraid you'd both get rusty!"

Mom laughed, sounding more cheerful. We chatted a little longer and then hung up.

I didn't mention the flare-up at Cotebrook to the others. There was every chance of it blowing over. All the same, I was concerned. Mom and Dad had worked hard to make the yard what it was. It was not right that some troublemaker should come along and ruin it all.

✳ ✳ ✳

Back in the office I brought up the subject of the camping ride.

"Good idea," Kate said. "We could take a crack at tracking down the wild herds. There's a chance we'll come across Cobweb's foal."

"That'd be great, but I'm not holding my breath. We'd never recognize it, for a start."

"We may not but I bet Cobweb would. Mares remember their foals for quite a while after they've been separated. It said so in the book on natural horsemanship I'm reading." Kate turned to Tom. "What about you, Tom? Are you coming?"

Tom was silent for a moment. Then he said, "I think you should leave this alone. You got Cobweb back. You could try for another foal out of her if that's what you want. I don't see the point in chasing after this one."

"But we're not," Kate argued. "We're going camping."

"What about this mess in the paper?" Tom said.

"What, the ghostly rider?" Kate curled a lip. "You don't honestly go along with all that?"

"I was thinking of Cobweb. It doesn't take much to set her off."

"It's OK," I said. "The ride will be a good experience for her."

"There you go, Tom. You're outnumbered. Do you want to come, or what?"

"Not particularly," Tom replied. "I promised Dad I'd work on the paperwork for the farm. And Cerys wants to go riding."

Kate's expression darkened. "Huh, I might have known Cerys Paige would factor into this somewhere! I wouldn't have thought she was your type."

"Cerys is just a friend," Tom said. "She's good company and you've got to hand it to her, she's a good rider. Merridance is going well and she was a skittish horse at first."

"Cerys was talking about replacing Merridance," I said.

"Was she?" Tom was surprised. "She never said anything to me. I thought she was fond of her."

"That type doesn't get fond of their horses," Kate said. "They get fed up with them and sell them. Why are boys so blind?"

The disagreement was in danger of turning into something more. I said hastily, "It doesn't matter if Tom's got other things going on. We can go by ourselves."

"OK," Kate said. "When would be best?"

"We'll need time to get our things together. Say, the day after tomorrow?"

"Great." Kate grinned. "I'll ask Mom to fix us some eats. I love camping, don't you? Nothing but the horses and us. Fantastic!"

That night, sleep was a long time coming. I lay staring into the darkness and puzzling matters over. I thought of the foal, now a yearling, that remained a blank image no matter how hard I tried to picture it. My sixth sense told me that it was alive and well, somewhere out there in the wilderness of the plains. But that was as far as it went. Where it was, or which herd it was with, evaded me completely.

I thought of Mom and Dad and wondered if they too were troubled and sleepless. My eyes were starting to grow heavy when a high, keening sound floating in through the open window brought me wide awake again. I sat up, flesh tingling. It came from the plain – the throbbing wail of a dog baying at the moon.

Or was it something else?

I got up and went to the window. A waning moon cast a feeble light over the farmyard and fields. In the paddocks, the three horses seemed unbothered. Zaide and Gold Brick stood nose to tail by their gate, dozing peacefully. Cobweb was grazing, her tail flicking now and again as she cropped the grass. There was no shadowy gray next to her. The howling had stopped.

All appeared as it should be… except that in their kennel the dogs had been disturbed. I could hear the clip-clip of their claws on the pavement as they paced up and down the length of their run. One of them gave a bothered little whine.

Next moment, there was a gentle tap on my door.

"Jenna, are you awake?" Kate's voice called softly.

"Yes. Come on in."

She entered the room, her hair all over the place, and headed straight for the window. "Something woke me up," she said, speaking quietly. "I wanted to make sure Zaide was all right. You can't see the paddocks from my room."

"Zaide's fine," I replied in the same hushed tones. "They all are. I was still awake and got up to check. Did you hear it?"

"Hear what?"

"The howling. It must have been what woke you."

"Oh, please!" Kate heaved a sigh. "I wish I hadn't mentioned that now. I might have known it would to set you off."

"What do you mean? *Set me off?* I don't imagine things. I heard it clearly."

Kate shrugged. "OK. Fine. It had to be one of the dogs. Taggle makes a howling noise in his throat if there's a fox around. It might be that."

"It wasn't Taggle. I know what he sounds like."

"Well, all right. Some other dog, then. Come on, Jenna. Don't glare at me like that."

"You don't believe me, do you? You think I'm making it up."

"I don't know what to believe. It's hard for people to get their heads around something they never experience themselves." She yawned widely. "I'm sleepy. I'm going back to bed. G'night."

I listened to her soft footfall on the landing, the creak of a loose floorboard, and then the connecting door that linked the gable room with the rest of the house closed with a click.

Frowning and annoyed with myself, I dived back into bed and pulled the comforter around me, wishing not for the first time that I could be more like Kate and Tom; practical and clear thinking, with my feet fixed firmly on the ground. After a while my eyes closed and I slept, only to be prowled by dreams of flying chariots, pounding horses, and the cold terror of two lean gray shapes loping along in pursuit.

It felt like an omen, for when I wakened I had changed my mind about going camping. Here within Broselake's thick stone walls was safety. Out on the plain, with just a flimsy tent between us and whatever lay beyond, who knew what might happen?

But when I went downstairs with the intention of telling Kate that the camping ride was off, I found her poring over the surveyor's map and marking out a route, and Meg was writing a list of supplies. Camping gear was piled all over the kitchen floor. On the table lay a computer printout provided by the mounted patrol, listing the spots where the plains herds were currently roaming.

My hopes sank. It seemed there was no backing out after all.

Chapter 8

"Cell phones," Meg said, writing it down.

Kate looked up from the map. "Is there any point? The signal's a bit iffy out there, Mom."

"I'm taking mine," I said, sitting at the table.

Tom, helping himself to cereal, glanced up and caught my gaze knowingly as if he suspected I was having second thoughts. He pushed the box of cereal across the table.

"Here. Enjoy. It'll be burned sausages starting tomorrow."

"Actually, I'm pretty good with a frying pan," I said.

"Frying pan," Meg echoed, scribbling. "I really think you should have your cell phone with you, Kate."

"OK," Kate said.

"What do you want to go on this crazy ride for, anyway?" Tom said. "You can get plenty of decent trail riding around here."

"Tom, cut it out," Kate told him fiercely. "We've had this ride planned for ages. Stop being creepy."

"I wasn't. I just don't think it's a great idea."

Meg put down her pencil. "Is there any reason for all this?"

"No," Kate said. "It's just Tom being Tom."

No one mentioned the howling in the night. I decided to forget it. Meg, still dubious, brought up the incident of the shepherd and his dog.

"He never did find out who the culprit was. Someone must have been pretty silly to go galloping around and frightening animals like that!"

"Oh, Mom!" Kate heaved a sigh. "You heard what the man said. There'd been hikers crossing the plain that day. It had to be them. Hikers do crazy things. It's a way of letting off steam."

Meg picked up the pencil and twiddled it thoughtfully.

"You could be right. Your dad spends half his life on the plain and he's never seen anything out of the ordinary. Oh well, let's see it for what it was – a silly prank. How long do you expect to be gone?"

Kate turned to me. "Two nights? Three? We should be able to cross the plain and be back again in that time. According to the patrol report we need to head out to Puck's Knowe and then go due north."

"That's uncharted territory," Tom said, crushingly.

"So what if it is?" Kate grinned at him. "We're ready for some adventure. I can't wait to try out the new camping gear. It's so lightweight the horses won't know they're carrying it. I think we should start out early, Jenna. It'll be cooler then."

A couple of nights wasn't too bad, I told myself, and putting aside my uneaten cereal, I went to pack.

✳ ✳ ✳

It was just after six when we mounted up, saddlebags and backpacks bulging with camping gear, changes of clothing, and food for ourselves and the horses. Zaide and Cobweb, fresh and eager to be off, stamped skittishly despite the extra weight they carried.

Daniel and Meg were loading up some ewes for market and Tom was not yet up. We rode out of the deserted farmyard with barely a word of goodbye, Gold Brick's plaintive whinnies ringing in our ears.

"Gold Brick hates being left behind," Kate said, leaning from the saddle to shut the yard gate with a clang. "You can't blame him, really. I think it's mean of Tom to duck out of coming. He was all for the idea before Cerys came along." She glanced around. "Sticky, isn't it? I thought it would be cooler but it isn't at all."

We passed the lake where the waters were molten under the yellow-white sky. Nothing stirred and the air was full of greenish light. It was as if the countryside was holding its breath. Flies buzzed in irritating swarms as we entered the tunnel of trees. We rode through the sleeping village, waving to the postman and then to a woman walking her dogs.

At the forge Ann Jenkins stood by the double doors, stretching and sniffing the air.

"Hi, you guys," she called out. "Going anywhere in particular?"

"The north plain," I shouted back, pulling up.

"Well, keep an eye on the weather. It feels like a storm to me."

106

"It's not forecasted," Kate said. "But we can always stop off somewhere for some shelter. There's Puck's Knowe. We should make it that far."

"Mind you keep away from the trees. I know lightning's never supposed to strike twice in the same place, but there's a history of trees being struck there." Ann ran a glance over the horses. "They're looking fit. How's Cobweb behaving? Eaten any more unsuspecting males lately?"

"Not that I know of," I said, laughing. "I think she's getting over it."

"Told you she would. Oh well, mustn't hold you up. Have fun, you two. Have a good time."

"We will," Kate said, legging on.

We made the first lap of the journey, stopping at around mid-morning to rest the horses and snack on the sandwiches Meg had prepared. The sun had still not come out; the sky was darkening ominously.

"That's not good," I said, frowning toward a yellowish bank of cloud on the horizon. "What about turning back?"

"Nah! We've got raincoats, and anyway, these freak storms never last long. What's Cobweb like in thunder?"

"She never used to mind it. What about Zaide?"

"Oh, it doesn't bother her. It's getting wet that she hates." Kate got up to tighten Zaide's girth, giving her neck a slap. "Sorry, girl, but you're about to get a soaking."

We had gone past Puck's Knowe and were heading northwards when the first heavy drops began. Thunder muttered in the distance. A zigzag of blue light pierced the sky, followed by another. Kate indicated a rocky outcrop that loomed out of the murk.

"That's our camping spot. Come on, we should make it before the storm breaks."

We reached the place just as the rain quickened. The campsite was one recommended by the endurance club and contained a large cave in the rock, made secure by solid wooden gates. Dismounting quickly, we hustled the horses inside, Zaide going in a rush to get out of the rain.

At the back of the cave was a stock of hay and straw and buckets for water.

"This is a great place to camp," Kate said. "Gary Robinson and some of the others put the gates up so the horses could be stabled safely during overnight stops."

I took in the solid walls and heavy gates and suggested, not with much hope, that we sleep inside with the horses.

"No need," Kate replied. "It'll pass over. I told you, these flash storms always do. Anyway, I want to try out the new gear." She winced at a particularly loud clap of thunder. "Doesn't look like we'll be putting the tent up for a while. We may as well get these two unsaddled."

We fed the horses a small amount of pony cubes from our supplies, adding hay from the store to keep them happy. Kate fished out a towel from her saddlebag and used it dry off her tack, throwing it to me to do the same.

"Do you want some juice? It'll help pass the time."

There were cookies, too. We munched on them and sat watching the storm, flinching when a bolt of light pierced the ground just outside the entrance. The horses laid back their ears and glanced around, wisps of hay hanging from their lips.

"That was close!" Kate said cheerfully. "We had a lightning strike at home once. It felled one of the trees in the orchard. The stump was actually burning. Tom wanted to take a photo of it, but by the time he'd found his camera the rain had started and put the fire out."

"Oh – don't!" I cried, giggly with nerves. "What about the lake? Does it ever flood?"

"It did last summer. We were OK at the farm because we're higher up, but we were marooned and couldn't get to school. Tom missed a gig he was supposed to be playing. Was he mad." Kate rolled her eyes dramatically.

For the next hour the thunder crashed and lightning crackled, filling the cave with blinding strobes of light. The rain pelted down.

"Remind me to call Mom afterwards," I said. "I meant to do it before we set off."

"Well, it *was* early."

"I know, but they'd have been up."

"Will you take over Cotebrook one day, do you think?" Kate asked, helping herself to an apple from the lunchbox.

"I'm not sure. It may not be there to take over."

"What do you mean?" Kate stared, apple halfway to her mouth.

"There's been some trouble. I don't think Mom's told me all of it. She wouldn't want to spoil the vacation."

"What sort of trouble?"

"An owner withdrew his horse. Then another called and cancelled. It was completely unexpected."

"Oh, that's awful!" Kate was horrified. "Do you have any idea why?"

"Not really. Mom said there was some gossip going around about Cobweb and the insurance. They're saying Mom and Dad were behind her disappearance, so they could put in a claim."

"That's crazy! Your folks wouldn't do anything so gross."

"Try telling the gossip-mongers that," I said. "No, of course they wouldn't. Dad kept the policy open in the hope that she'd turn up again."

"Which she did. So where's the problem?"

"Oh, you know how it is. Some people are born troublemakers. The thing is, you never know how far the gossip will spread. Mom sounded really upset last night."

"I'm not surprised. Who on earth could be behind it all?"

"I don't know. It could be anyone. You make enemies when you're successful."

Just then, Kate's cell phone jangled to indicate a text. It was Meg, wanting to know if we were all right and saying the river had burst its bank and half of Ravensmoor was under water.

"It always happens when it rains like this," Kate said, sending an answer. "The water takes a long time to go down because the village is low-lying."

"Good thing we didn't turn back, then."

"We'd have needed to take the long way around, and there's no way of knowing whether that would have been any better. I'd never get Zaide through floods, no way. There…" She put her cell phone aside. "I told Mom where we are and we're OK. I wish she wouldn't worry. It isn't as if we're new to camping."

As quickly as it had come the wild summer storm died away. The clouds parted and the sun broke through. The whole face of the plain began to steam and the air was full of gurgling and slapping as the swollen streams raced toward the river.

"Come on." Kate stood up. "Let's tether the horses outside and let them get some grass. One good thing; the rain will clear the air. I hate the heat. It makes me grumpy."

"I noticed."

"Sorry." She grinned. "I wonder how the others did? They were riding to some yard or other to find a new horse for Cerys. I hope they got completely drenched and it ruined her hair!"

✳ ✳ ✳

Afterwards, once the tent was up and camping gear sorted, we went to explore. This outcrop could not have been more different from Puck's Knowe. Birds twittered happily in the trees and rabbits had made their dens in the sandy banks. The spring that bubbled up out of the ground was clear and sparkling. There was no hint of desolation or gloom. The place was as normal as could be.

Shadows were long when we arrived back at the camp. We cooked sausages over the camp stove and ate them hungrily, finishing off with fruit and some chocolate which Meg had packed in an ice pack to prevent it from melting.

Supper over, I pulled out my cell phone. "I wonder if I can get a decent signal on this."

"You can always try. Sending the text was a little tricky before." Kate was leaning her back against a rock, eyes closed, relaxed and sleepy. "You might stand a better chance on the hillside. Good luck. You never know, the problems may have gotten sorted out."

But when, after scrambling over some loose pebbles on the side of the rock face, I managed to get through to Cotebrook, it was Dad who answered and he sounded grim.

"Hi, Jenna. How's Cobweb? Not acting up too much?"

"We've had our moments. Nothing I couldn't cope with. We're camping right now."

"What, in the storm? I heard it's been bad over your way."

The signal was not good. Dad's voice stuttered on and off.

"We found a shelter," I told him. "It's been fine."

"What's that? I can't hear you very well."

I moved further up the slope, my feet slithering on the shale. "Is that better? Great. Dad, Mom mentioned a problem on the yard. What's been going on?"

I heard him catch his breath. "I only wish I knew. How much did Mom tell you?"

"Only that there was a nasty rumor going around and Carter Harrison had taken his filly to another trainer. Oh, and that you'd had a cancellation."

"And the rest," Dad said bitterly.

I braced myself. Dad always spoke to me as an equal and he did so now.

112

"It all blew up out of nowhere. One moment we had as much work as we could cope with, the next thing the place was emptying fast. Owners called wanting to pull their horses out. Nothing I could say would stop them."

I swallowed hard. Our livelihood depended on the income from the horses we trained. Without it, the yard could not function.

"How many have gone?"

"All six. The only animals here now are our own. I may have to sell one of the yearlings to keep us afloat."

"Dad, you can't! The young stock is our future. You're always saying that."

"Any more glitches like this one and Cotebrook won't have a future! I'm sorry, Jenna. I'm afraid there's no choice."

Dad sounded utterly stressed out.

"Have you looked into how the rumors started?" I asked him.

"I've tried. As far as I can tell Carter Harrison was out for a meal with friends and overheard a conversation about Cotebrook. What was said wasn't very pleasant."

"But Mr. Harrison knows us. So why did he believe it?"

"Because it's how people are. They go into panic mode. We're not the only yard in the business. There are lots of other trainers that do a pretty good job at schooling a horse. This owner wasn't taking any risks. Maybe in his place I'd have done the same thing."

"I don't think so," I said stoutly. "You'd have investigated it first."

"I think he tried, but by then the gossip was growing and his best option seemed to pull out. Anyway, I made it clear that we were in no way responsible for what was being said and left it at that. We had to return his fee, naturally."

I bit my lip. Payment for having a horse trained was given three months in advance. The fee was hefty. This, added to all the other animals that had left, would mean a big loss in funds.

"What are you going to do?" I asked in a low voice.

"Soldier on. Something will turn up." Dad paused. "Sorry to burden you with all this, Jenna. Mom told me not to spoil your fun, but you have to know sometime."

"Yes." I didn't know what else to say. "Do you want me to come home?"

"No, of course not. You stay where you are. I can't think of a better place to be."

Despite everything, I laughed. "Right now I'm perched on a slippery rock face and it's getting dark."

"Oops! For a moment I'd forgotten you weren't at the farm. What's the idea? Trying to figure out where Cobweb's foal is?"

"How did you guess?"

"It wasn't difficult. Just watch out if you come across the herds. They're an unpredictable bunch… Oh, there's your Mom. Better go – unless you want to talk to her?"

"Not now. I'll have to go while I can still see my way. Give Mom my love. Tell her I'll try and call tomorrow. If you don't hear from me it's because of the signal."

"OK. Try not to let this get you down. 'Bye, Jenna. Love you."

Thoughtfully I picked my way down the slope and, guided by the glow of the lamp that Kate had lit, returned to the camp.

"It's not good news, judging from your face," she said. "We'd better stable the horses, and then you can tell me all about it."

Unfastening the tethers, we led Zaide and Cobweb back to the cave.

"Be good," I said, taking off Cobweb's head collar and turning her loose.

"Same goes for you, Zaide," Kate added.

We left them with some hay and fresh water from the spring and returned to the tent, sitting down at the entrance. The plain was now wrapped in darkness. In the distance, the high peak of Mani's Finger made a stark outline against the sky. Above, a sickle moon sailed serenely among its company of stars.

I told Kate the news from home.

"But that's ridiculous!" she cried. "Everyone knows your yard is the best. How can people be so stupid?"

"I don't know. Dad sounded really upset."

I drew a shuddering breath, staring ahead. All at once I stiffened. A light had appeared in the far distance. It seemed to be traveling slowly.

"What's that? A light of some sort. Over there near Puck's Knowe."

As I was speaking the light flickered and vanished.

"I don't see anything," Kate said.

"It's gone now. How weird."

"Dad's seen fireflies and will-o'-the-wisps on the plain, especially after it's rained. It could have been either of those."

"No." I shook my head. "It was moving, like it was someone with a flashlight."

"Well, there's nothing there now." Kate sent the silent landscape another frowning glance. "The plain can be creepy at night. Maybe we should have brought one of the dogs with us. Dad did offer. I almost wish I hadn't turned him down."

"Now she tells me!"

"Oh, it was probably nothing." Kate yawned widely. "I'm exhausted. Let's turn in, OK?"

We settled down for the night and were soon asleep.

Cantering through my dreams went the herds of ponies we were hoping to trace. Squeals and whinnies and their drumming flight hammered on my brain, and at some point in the night the dream became reality. I was roused from a deep sleep by Cobweb calling shrilly from the cave. It was followed by Zaide's deeper tones. I heard the scraping of iron-shod hooves on the rocky floor as the two of them roamed the confines of their stable.

For a moment I lay there, my thoughts spinning chaotically. I couldn't make out what was wrong. And then I heard what must have disturbed them... the rhythmic thudding of hoofbeats out there on the plain.

Beside me, Kate slept on.

"Kate!" I shook her hard. "Wake up."

"Whazamatter?"

"Get up!" I hissed, reaching for my clothes. "There's something going on out there."

Zaide let out another piercing shout. Kate came instantly awake.

"That's Zaide! What's happening? Where are my things?"

Before Kate had got herself together I was dressed and out, scrambling up the slithery slope where there was a better view. The moon was higher, its crescent not giving much light, but the stars shone brilliantly and in their gleam I saw a figure galloping across the plain. The horse was big and powerful and the rider's long garments and rippling hair streamed out behind her glimmering strangely in the darkness.

I stared, unable to believe what I saw. Around me, the plain felt vast and threatening. There was nowhere to run to, nowhere to hide and I stood helpless, wishing I were anywhere but here.

Chapter 9

"Jenna, what's going on?"

Kate came panting up beside me, her feet slithering on the loose pebbles of the rock face. She gazed at the spectacle in disbelief. "W...wow!"

From the cave below came another ear-splitting whinny. We watched as the rider gained the stark outline of Puck's Knowe and vanished from view.

"Did I really see that?" Kate said in a voice that wobbled.

No sooner were the words out when a high-pitched, eerie wailing came to us on the night wind. It rose and fell, rippling across the rolling vista of plains, before slowly fading away. Everywhere now lay still and silent under the stars.

Kate, her face white in the darkness, clutched my arm. "What... what was that?"

"I don't know," I said.

Now that I was over my initial shock I was frantically trying to figure it all out. One thing was certain: what we had seen and heard was no phantom. But Kate was obviously scared and I tried to reassure her.

"It's got to be like you said – someone out there fooling around."

"But why would they? That horse could have gone down and broken a leg. What sort of rider would risk that? And where did those howls come from?"

"Sound carries at night. Maybe it was a farm dog."

Kate sent me a look of utter scorn. "Jenna, that was no dog!"

"Well, whatever it was it's stopped now. We'd better see if Zaide and Cobweb are all right."

Kate followed me in silence down the slope and by the time we reached the cave she seemed more in control. The horses greeted us with anxious whickers. The water buckets had been knocked over and the sandy floor was trampled where they had paced. Now, they stood contrite by the gate. We refilled the buckets and hay nets and watched as they inspected this unaccustomed midnight feast.

"They should be all right now," Kate said. "Do you have any idea what time it is?"

I glanced at my watch. "Twelve o'clock. We may as well go back to bed."

"OK," Kate said.

Neither of us slept much. We lay talking about what had happened, while above the moon sailed innocently on her journey across the sky. I stuck to my theory that it was some idiot masquerading as Mani the legendary goddess, and Kate argued that no one in their right mind would risk harming a horse with such a stupid act. And she was probably right.

We were up at the first twitter of birds, dismantling

the tent and breakfasting on fruit from our supplies, since neither of us wanted to stay around long enough to cook something. At the back of the cave was an assortment of stable tools. We mucked out, emptied the water buckets and, satisfied that the place was just as we had found it, we loaded up our gear and set off, yawning and heavy-eyed from the night's broken sleep.

Crossing the high plain generally took two full days of serious riding. Our route was mapped out for the quickest way – but we had calculated without yesterday's storm. Once we reached the lower levels of the north plain we found, instead of the expected gulley that could have been easily crossed, a vast, glittering lake of floodwater.

"Typical!" Kate muttered.

Zaide's ears almost met at the tips. She gave a ferocious snort and started to back away from the wavelets that threatened to wash her hooves. Cobweb, always up for anything, pawed the ground in excitement.

"You must have been a water buffalo in another life!" I said, patting her arching neck. I turned to Kate. "What should we do? Try wading across?"

"You're joking! I'd never get Zaide across. Anyway, it looks a little deep for that. I think we'd better try a different route."

Kate pulled the map from her saddlebag and studied it. "OK. From here we go due west and pick up the other trail. That'll take us a lot further north than we intended." She made a face. "It'll add several hours on the journey. Still, there is a place to camp so that's something."

We rode on, skirting the floodwater, our backs now to the sun. This part of the plain was starred with tiny flowers and the horses' hooves released puffs of pollen that rose in spiraling clouds around us. My eyes began to water; my nose tickled, and soon I was having a spectacular sneezing attack that made the horses flick their ears in shock.

"We should have brought some antihistamines," Kate said.

"Oh, it'll stop on its own." I mopped streaming eyes. "It was worse when I was little. At one time Mom never thought I'd be able to have a pony of my own."

"That's terrible!" Kate bit her lip, then said, "I wonder how things are at your place."

"I wouldn't know. I'll give them a call later on."

"We're a long way from a cell tower now. You may have to wait till we get to Milton."

That was the village where we planned to stock up on supplies for the homeward ride, now a good deal farther away than we had planned.

"I keep thinking about that rider," Kate went on. "It was scary. That howling gave me goose bumps. I can't imagine how I slept through it all."

"We were dead tired. I think it must have been going on for quite a while. I'd been dreaming and sort of hearing noises at the same time. If Cobweb hadn't made such a racket I might not have woken up either."

It struck me then that this was how I had been so certain that what we saw was a fake. Anything else, anything more otherworldly, and I would have awakened at once.

Cobweb was walking on a loose rein, relaxed and easy, and I ran a hand along her flank that was now taking on the gloss that comes from regular grooming. Just then the horses' heads came up. Their ears were pricked. Cobweb, quivering in excitement, made a breathy little whicker.

"See over there," Kate whispered. "Ponies!"

They were grazing some distance away, a small herd of mares, foals and yearlings, the stallion in their midst. Zaide began to prance and skitter and Cobweb started spinning around in demented circles. Kate brought Zaide instantly under control, but Cobweb took longer, and it was a while before she was quiet enough for me to take a serious look at the herd, standing up in my stirrups for a better view.

"They're too far away to see properly," Kate said, keeping her voice low. "I bet if we try and get closer they'll take off."

"That's the trouble. Cobweb doesn't seem to recognize any of them. Her foal can't be there." I was quivery with disappointment.

"True. Oh well, let's keep going. We're sure to come across others."

We pressed on, leaving the grazing herd behind. At noon we stopped for a break, letting the horses graze while we ate the last of our sandwiches – a little dry but still good – and drank bottled water.

Kate got out the map and sat frowning over it.

"How far is it to the campsite?" I asked.

"Another three hours' ride, I think. See here?" She pointed to a marked spot on the map. "This is where we should have camped. It's close to Milton. And this is where we're heading – a long way off."

On the plus side, the campsite had a belt of leafy woodland and a deep freshwater pool.

"It might be OK," I said. "We'll be able to swim in the pool."

"That's a thought. I just hope the food lasts, that's all." Kate was rummaging anxiously through her pockets. "My cell phone! It's not here!"

"It must be. When did you have it last?"

"Yesterday in the cave, when I sent that text home. I put it down on the ledge by the gates. This morning we were in such a hurry to leave I completely forgot about it. Drat! I know the signal's bad here, but I thought I'd try and get hold of Mom to tell her about the change of route."

"Do you want to use mine?"

"No, it's OK, thanks. We can do it when we get to Milton. Remind me to pick my cell phone up on the way back."

Soon we were on our way again, my occasional sneeze piercing the quiet, the horses taking offense and flicking their ears. All life on the plain drowsed in the hot afternoon sun. Bees buzzed in the heather and crickets chirruped monotonously from their secret haunts in the turf. High above, a red-tailed hawk wheeled in lazy circles in the blue.

We saw no more wild ponies; the prospect of coming across the foal grew depressingly dim. Time seemed to hang suspended. There was nothing but the flanks of the open plain, the sleepy hum of insects and the endless arch of sky. Then, just as it seemed that the ride would never end, a row of trees came into view.

At once I stiffened in the saddle, my gaze riveted to the straggly line of greenery that edged the plain. I had seen the same scene before, flashed into the dark corner of a stable by a hand from another time. My heart started to quake and thump; my hands felt sweaty on the reins. Part of me wanted to turn and ride away as fast as we could. But I was curious too, and for some reason I could not understand why I felt driven to go on. I had no idea. I just knew I must.

"That place ahead has to be the campsite," I said, trying to sound normal even though dread was pounding through me.

"Great." Kate, unknowing, kicked her feet from the stirrups and stretched her aching legs. "Don't know about you, but I'm ready to get out of the saddle."

"Me too." I threw a glance over my shoulder. "Kate, did you hear anything?"

"Like what?"

"Like another horse? I get the feeling we're being followed."

I'd heard hoofbeats, I was sure.

"Oh, come on!" Kate said irritably, snatching a brief look around. "There's absolutely nothing there and you can see for miles. Of course we're not being followed."

"Grump."

"Grump yourself!"

She gave in with a grin and we arrived at the edge of the woods. It was cooler under the trees and we followed a winding path, looking for the pool and a place to camp, Cobweb spooking at hidden rustlings in the undergrowth. She hadn't liked being among trees since her time away.

We had gone deep into the heart of the woods when voices rang out unexpectedly. They were angry and threatening and we pulled up in alarm. The voices came from beyond a screen of bushy evergreens, a man and a woman, arguing fiercely.

"I'm sick of hanging around here! The sooner this lot's shipped off the better," the woman cried.

"Oh, give it a break, Stacey!" the man replied. "It was your choice to make this one last deal. If it wasn't for that we'd be gone by now, relaxing somewhere in the sun."

"Don't give me that, Bart Jones! You were the one to set the targets. Thirty, you said, then we stop. This lot will round that off nicely."

"That's assuming things go OK. I never liked shipping animals out of the country. Too many things can go wrong."

"Of course it'll be OK. We've had no problems so far. Oh, what's the point in arguing. Only a few more days to go, then we're through."

There was a pause, and then the woman said, "You'd better water those ponies, Bart, unless you want them to flake out with thirst."

Cobweb's ears had flattened. She started to tremble and I stroked her neck soothingly. I was about to ride on when Kate put out a hand to stop me, indicating the row of bushes that screened the speakers from view.

"Let's see what's going on over there," she whispered.

Dismounting, we led the horses and crept forward, gingerly parting the branches.

In a clearing beyond was a rough-made enclosure containing six ponies – yearlings, by the look of them. They were leggy creatures, wide-eyed, innocent, and patched all over with tufts of fuzzy black foal coat that they were in the process of outgrowing.

One of them was going to be a bright, burnished bay.

A woman in jeans and a skimpy top sat on the steps of a battered and rusted mobile home, raking her fingers through her long dark hair and talking to a thickset man dressed in army camouflage. Close to them on the trail, a four-wheel-drive was loaded up with luggage. At the head of the clearing stood a small chalet-type building, which could once have been a ranger's hut when this section of the plain was permanently manned. Changes in management and a switch to a central patrolling body had made these individual ranger stations defunct a long time ago.

The man pulled himself up, sauntered over to where a stream gurgled through the trees, and after filling a bucket with water he returned and offered it to the yearlings. They clamored around, pushing and shoving, desperate to drink.

"That's all you're getting!" the man growled, rattling the empty bucket at them. The nearest pony plunged back with a cry of distress and the whole group swept off to the furthest corner of the stockade, where they stood trembling and rolling their eyes in fright.

"You shouldn't do that, Bart. It'll make them head-shy," the woman said.

"So what if it does? Won't be our problem, will it? Stupid creatures. They're all teeth and hooves. You never know which end to watch out for."

The woman shrugged, scooping up her hair indifferently and securing it with a cheap plastic clip. "A little kindness helps. Not that you'd know much about that…"

We stared, open-mouthed. Kate's face was scarlet with suppressed fury. The man was a tough-looking character with buzz-cut hair and mean little eyes in a jowly face. Somewhere on the edge of my mind it registered that he might be the cause of Cobweb's uncertain attitude toward men in general.

Crouched there among the dust-laden bushes, my sinuses began once again to react. In desperation I pegged my fingers over my nose to stop the sneezing fit I knew was coming – but it was useless. A spluttering sneeze escaped me, then another. The man looked around.

"What was that?"

The woman had leaped to her feet and was running

in our direction, shouting as she went. "Don't just stand there you fool! There's someone there!"

"Quick!" Kate said. "Let's get out of here."

She hiked up into the saddle, yanked Zaide around and went galloping off down the path, camping gear rattling alarmingly. I tried to do the same – but Cobweb had seen the yearlings. Whinnying, she started to pull violently against the tight rein I held her by. A little bay answered her and Cobweb fought me all the more.

"Stand!" I begged her. "Whoa, girl! Stand!"

It was useless. Footsteps came crashing through the undergrowth. I made one desperate leap for the saddle – too late. Panting breath assailed me. One big red hand seized Cobweb's reins and the other fastened itself with a vice-like grip on my arm.

"Gotcha!" the man snarled. "This way!"

"No!" I screamed. "Let go of me! Let go!"

Kate must have realized I was not following and came back to see what was wrong. When she saw what had happened her face registered sheer horror.

"Jenna! Oh, Jenna!" she gasped.

"Hey, Stacey, there's another one!" the man hollered. "Get the horse and go after her, or we're done for!"

"Kate!" I yelled. "Get away! Go on!"

Throwing me one last despairing glance, Kate shouted something I could not catch and sent Zaide thundering off, while I was frog-marched, protesting and struggling, into the clearing.

"Let go of me! You're hurting me! Let me go, you pig!"

I might as well have saved my breath. Bart, an ugly leer on his face, only tightened his grip. Cobweb was now in a frenzy of fear, fighting and plunging against the hand that held her. Swearing under his breath and without relinquishing his hold on my arm, Bart flung the reins over the gatepost of the stockade.

The bay filly had been tearing up and down the fence with the others and calling out for what had to be her mother. She now joined Cobweb, and in all the chaos and confusion the two made a joyful reunion through the rails, whickering and nibbling, while the other captives continued to plunge around, their hard little hooves creating clouds of dust in the narrow confines of their enclosure.

The woman was throwing a saddle on a big steel-gray gelding that was tethered on a patch of grass by the mobile home. She then had to replace the head collar with a bridle. Clumsy in her haste, the minutes were ticking by, and by the time she was mounted and giving the horse its head it looked encouragingly as if Kate had made her escape.

Bart spat out a curse and turned his vengeance on me. "Interfering little busybody! Trouble-shooting little snoop! There's only one place for the likes of you!"

I fought him, kicking, biting, anything to get free, but his hold was firm. The door of the hut was jerked open. I was flung inside, pitching headlong onto the wooden floor with a force that dealt the side of my head a ringing blow. The door slammed shut behind me and, fighting waves of dizziness and nausea, I heard the rattle of heavy iron bolts being shot home.

I was alone in the blackest dark, with Cobweb at the mercy of those two thugs. Things couldn't have gotten much worse, and tears of pure helplessness and frustration welled and rolled silently onto the dusty floor of my prison.

Chapter 10

I don't know how long I lay there in the stifling heat of the hut. My arm, which had lost circulation gradually, revived in agonizing spasms of pins and needles. My head was thumping and my arm throbbed with a deadly ache, but after a while the pins and needles stopped and I could feel my fingers again.

Very cautiously I pulled myself up to a sitting position, removed my riding hat and ran an exploratory finger over my sore temple. Except for a graze and a slight bump, it did not feel too bad. I wondered dully how Cobweb was and if she had been put in the stockade with the others.

Hoofbeats thudded out suddenly from the clearing beyond. The woman had returned – empty-handed, it seemed. Breath held, I listened to what she said.

"It was another girl. She got away. Wow, could that mare travel! It was an Arab, I think. Wouldn't mind a foal out of that one."

"I thought you couldn't wait to get away." Bart sounded exasperated.

"So? That one was pure gold."

"Oh, forget it, Stacey! We've been at this game for

long enough. We've made a decent wad out of this, so let's stop now."

"We don't have any choice, do we? Bart, we'll have to decide what to do. That girl's sure to raise the alarm."

"We've got time on our side. We're nowhere near civilization here. She's not likely to contact anyone in a hurry."

"She could have a cell phone on her. OK, so the signal's iffy, but you never know."

"You're right." Bart cursed roundly. "We'd better check the other one."

Footsteps came pounding toward the shed. The bolts were drawn, the door flung open, letting in a blinding beam of daylight. My captors came storming in.

"On your feet, kid! You got a cell phone? Search her, Stacey."

In seconds the slim-line phone in my jodhpurs pocket was discovered and handed over. Dropping it to the floor, Bart raised his booted foot and brought it smashing down, rendering what had been a much-treasured birthday present from Gran to a mess of crushed plastic at my feet.

"Don't want to take any chances, do we?" Bart said nastily.

Sickening bands of pain engulfed my head. The hut swam momentarily around me. I thought vaguely about a concussion and wondered what was happening with Kate. She had a long trek ahead of her to raise the alarm. Would she make for the cave and her lost cell phone or head for Milton? Either way would take time. I had an uneasy feeling that time was not on my side.

"She doesn't look good, Bart." The woman looked me over closely. "I'd better find something for that bump on her temple. Want a drink, kid?"

I shrugged. I had a raging thirst but I didn't want any favors from those two and my lips remained stubbornly closed.

"Weren't you taught any manners?" Bart said. "Answer when you're spoken to!"

I sent the woman a nod that sent a fresh dagger of pain across my forehead. Through the open doorway I could see Cobweb's saddle and bridle lying in the dust where it had been thrown, along with my camping gear. Cobweb was in the stockade with the other ponies, the bay yearling glued to her side. They were all circling the fence restlessly.

"Don't get any ideas about making a run for it," Bart cautioned. "'Cause you wouldn't stand a chance."

Stacey left and was soon back with a plastic beaker of water and a dampened cloth that smelled of antiseptic. "Here, drink up and mop your head with this."

Taking the water, I forced myself to sip it down slowly. Then I dabbed at my face with the cloth; the antiseptic stung and made my eyes weep.

Bart jerked his head in the direction of the door, indicating to his companion for them to leave. Without another word Stacey took the empty beaker and the cloth from me and followed him out, securing the door behind them.

I sank to the floor with my back to the wall, hugging my knees. The water had been refreshing and I felt slightly better. My head still throbbed, though not with quite the same intensity.

I tried to come up with a plan.

After a while I got up, and feeling my way around the walls I came across a single small window that was boarded up. One corner felt loose and I worked at it, pulling at the plank of wood. The frame was rotten and a section came away, letting in a welcome stream of fresh air and daylight.

Glancing around, I saw that the hut was bare except for a pile of junk in one corner. I went to investigate it, hoping for something that might help me escape. But the search revealed only some moldy horse blankets, a few used meal cartons and what seemed like a bundle of rags, which turned out to be a moth-eaten assortment of fancy dress clothes. Gingerly I held up a shapeless garment covered with silvery daubs, throwing it down again in disgust. Nothing here was any use to me.

Going back to the window, I tried to free the remaining boards, but the nails held fast, and anyway the opening was too small to climb through. So taking the precaution of easing back the loosened planking over the gap, I sat down again.

The activity had left me strangely exhausted and unable to think clearly. Random pieces of what had happened went flitting through my mind, vivid, disjointed.

Puck's Knowe, the light moving in the darkness, the

reckless midnight rider… the row of trees I had seen before in the time-wind, that weird sensation of being followed that had come over me as we crossed the north plain. And running relentlessly through the jumble of thoughts went the high, eerie music of the wolf pack. It all had to be connected, but in my fuddled state none of it made much sense.

What was obvious was that the two thugs outside were behind the racket that had caused Cobweb and other top mares to vanish for a time and turn up again, after having had a foal which the rustlers had kept for their own use. Stacey had mentioned the current stock being "shipped off" at some point, so they evidently had an outlet for what they were doing. It seemed incredible that they had not been discovered before now. But then I recalled the sheer vastness of the plain, the many isolated pockets like this one that made perfect hiding places, the lack of regular official patrols… all so ideal for a scheme like this. And I realized with a horrible sinking feeling that if help did not come soon I ran the risk of losing Cobweb's foal for good.

Time passed. An hour. Two. I wondered if Kate had contacted Emergency Services yet. She would have dumped the saddlebags, giving them more speed. Even so, no horse could gallop indefinitely.

Outside, dusk was falling. There was a smell of cooking, a curry of some kind. No one brought me any food. It sounded as if the rustlers were eating on the steps of the mobile home, since their talk drifted.

"Those two kids must have been the campers I told you about," Stacey said.

"The ones near Puck's Knowe? Huh, fine job you did of scaring them off!" Bart was scornful. "What about the sound system I set up? Did you make sure to activate it?"

"Yeah, of course I did. Talk about howls! Those kids must have nerves of steel."

Everything slid inexorably into place. I shot a glance at the corner and the musty pile of dress up clothes. It was so obvious I felt stupid at not having figured it out for myself. The ghostly rider facade had been nothing more than a ruse to keep people away so that the horse thieves could get on with their business undisturbed. It was a simple but brilliantly clever trick, for there was nothing more likely to stir fear into the hearts of superstitious plains folk than the threat of Mani and her moon horses returning to haunt the countryside. It looked as if Kate and I had unwittingly stumbled upon the rustling scam of the century!

The couple went on discussing what they should do next.

"I've been in touch with the others and told them we need to hurry things up," Stacey said. "We moved the collection date up. The ponies are being picked up in the morning at first light. Then we can get away."

"I still think we're taking a chance, staying here." Bart was speaking with his mouth full and the words came out garbled. "Why don't we go now while we can?"

"Because of the payment. Think of the money we'd be throwing away."

"I'd rather think of my freedom. We're not exactly broke. We've got enough stashed away to live very comfortably."

"So this final payment is the icing on the cake. We'd be crazy to leave without it. Only a few more hours and we'll be on our way… and we'll have the cash in our pockets."

There was a pause, into which came the munching of the gelding as he cropped the rank woodland grass. Then Stacey said, "What about the mare? We can't let her go with the others. There's a risk she'll be identified. We'll have to turn her loose."

"Nah! You can leave that side of things to me."

"And the girl?"

"I'll deal with her too," Bart said darkly.

My insides churned. I thought of the stories of people and animals perishing in the bottomless pockets of plains bogs, and swallowed a gulp of fear.

Stacey spoke again. "We might consider a ransom. The kid must have folks who'll be worrying about her. What if we put a price on her head?"

"What if you get some common sense?" Bart challenged. "I never did like ransom. My way's better."

Please, please, someone help me! I prayed, fervently and silently.

There was the clatter of dishes being collected, the sound of a door closing, and then quiet.

The night drew on. Deep in the woods an owl hooted to its mate and was answered. Now and then there was a spluttering snort from the stockade, the stamp of a restless hoof, the scratching of a mouse under the floorboards. Soon, the sky would lighten toward the dawn, and then what?

Curling up on the bare floor, I closed my eyes, my plea for help a mantra on my lips. I must have dozed; the dream when it came was so clear it might have been real.

I was flying in mist. There was chanting, the drumbeat of hooves, and then I was out of the vapor and sailing through starry skies toward the bright arc of a new moon. A voice was calling out to me, a well-remembered voice, and yet the speaker when she appeared was not as I had imagined her to be. She was not much taller than me but her upright bearing and proud carriage gave the impression of height and authority. Swathes of moon-gold hair swirled about her, eddied by the time-wind that had brought her here. I stared into her strong face, at the firm chin, the hooked nose and slightly cruel set of the mouth, all of which should have been scary, but I saw how her eyes regarded me with nothing but respect and compassion.

She reached out to touch me… but already the dream was fading as dreams do. The midnight skies and reeling moonlight began to fracture; the figure melted away, and I was alone once more in the wreathing blanket of mist. Alone, yet curiously reassured that help was at hand.

Stirring where I lay on the hard floor, I stretched stiffened limbs and came abruptly awake to a light scratching sound at the boarded-up window.

"Jenna?" whispered a voice that was wonderfully, impossibly, familiar.

"Tom?" Scrambling up, I stumbled to the window. "Oh, Tom! Is it really you?"

"Shh! Not so loud. Of course it's me. Listen. The door isn't padlocked. I'm coming in."

Tom slinked shadow-like to the front of the building and, releasing the bolts with a scraping sound that grated chillingly on the night, he let himself into the hut. Laughing and sobbing at once I threw myself at him, and Tom patted my back reassuringly and told me to get a grip, otherwise those two thugs out there might hear and then we'd both be goners.

Once I was calmer, Tom, speaking softly, explained how he came to be here.

"I've been trying to catch up with the two of you. Cerys … oh, never mind that now. I came across Kate on the plain, galloping as if wolves were chasing her. She told me what had happened. I sent a message to the authorities, just hope it got through. Kate's back there now with the horses."

"Tom, they've got Cobweb. Her foal's here as well. It's a rustler gang."

"I know. I've been out there, waiting for things to get quiet. I expected them to push off while the coast was clear."

"No, they want the payment for the yearlings. Someone's coming for them very early in the morning. The truck could turn up any time. The… the man had other plans for Cobweb and me."

Tom's face was a pale blur in the dimness, but I

heard his quick intake of breath and his arm tightened protectively around my shoulders.

"Listen, I think we should get out of here fast."

"I'm not leaving Cobweb!"

"Nobody's expecting you to. It might be best if you went and got her. She'll only kick up a fuss if I do it. The foal should follow. Ready? Quiet as you can."

Moving stealthily we went out of the airless heat of the hut into the cool, dewy night. Cobweb's bridle and saddle were still on the ground where they had been thrown. The saddlebags had been ransacked; the contents lay strewn in the dust.

The ponies had seen us and began milling around. Tom, darting a cautious glance at the shuttered mobile home, picked up the tack and handed me the bridle, putting a finger to his lips to indicate silence. Hardly daring to breathe, I let myself into the stockade, dodging a colt that was quick to show his heels.

Cobweb must have known what was at stake and allowed herself to be caught with no trouble. I attached the bridle and led her out, the bay filly dancing nervously at her side. Tom had put the saddle on the railings. I put it on and fastened the girth, my fingers rubbery with nerves.

The yearlings were still moving around apprehensively, their little hooves chinking against loose stones in the churned muck and dust of the stockade, eyes glinting white in the darkness. All at once, one of them let out a loud whinny. Almost immediately a light went on in the mobile home.

"They're onto us," Tom hissed. "Quick. Get up!"

He boosted me up into the saddle as the door opened and Bart and Stacey came stumbling out, still in their daytime clothes and rubbing the sleep from their eyes.

"Hey, you!" Bart hollered. "What do you think you're doing?"

"Go on, Jenna," Tom cried.

He landed a thump on Cobweb's quarters that sent her and the filly plunging into the cover of the trees. But I wasn't leaving Tom to face those two on his own. Pulling up, I swung Cobweb around and urged her back into the clearing.

Tom and Bart were wrestling on the ground. Thuds and punches and the grunts of violent combat grated on the air. In the stockade, the yearlings charged up and down squealing in fright. Tom was young and fit but he was no match for the burly rustler and Stacey was there, armed with a stout stick, ready to aim it if need be.

"Leave him alone!" I shrieked, wheeling Cobweb around to hold the woman off. Stacey wielded the stick threateningly and Cobweb, going up in a half-rear, started to fight me, tossing her head, dropping a shoulder, anything to take off with me and escape. The filly darted about determinedly at her side, refusing to be parted no matter what.

Tightening my grip, I rode again at my opponent, yelling madly.

"Get away! Get away!" And then, in desperation, "OH, HELP US, SOMEBODY!"

Someone heard.

Above the clamor of the fighting and the frightened calls of the ponies came a shrill blast of whinnies and the hammer of powerful hooves, and the horse appeared out of the night. Muscled and hardy, his eyes flashing and nostrils flaring, the great gray stallion screamed his vengeance and hurled himself at the wrestling trio. The woman dropped her weapon and fled. Bart, confronted with an unexpected barrage of flailing forehooves and gnashing teeth, staggered back in shock.

Tom pulled himself to his feet. He cast one disbelieving look at his attacker, and then made a dive for me.

"Go!" he gasped. "I'm right behind you!"

Close to panic I turned Cobweb toward the trees and let her go, the bay filly streaking alongside. I was beginning to feel very strange. My head jabbed painfully with every pounding stride. There was a buzzing in my ears and the flashing trunks of the trees started to waver and grow fuzzy. We made it through the woods and out into the open where Kate waited, mounted on Zaide and holding Gold Brick's reins.

"Jenna! Thank goodness," she cried.

Tom came sprinting out of the woods behind us. At the same time the plain seemed to erupt into noise and bands of flashing blue light. As if from a long way off I heard the unmistakable drone of an air rescue helicopter and saw, cantering toward us, the shapes of the horses and the uniformed men of the mounted patrol.

My heart was hammering so violently I could hardly breathe. I tried to speak, felt myself sliding from the saddle, and everything fell away into blackness.

Chapter 11

"Some camping ride that turned out to be!"

Mom gave her head a rueful shake, but she was smiling. At her side Dad was regarding me with the same curious mixture of admonishment and pride. We were in the big, comfortable lounge at Broselake. I was sitting opposite them on the sofa, Tom and Kate on either side. Daniel had just come in with the dogs and Meg was handing out coffee and chocolate cake.

"You three certainly don't do things halfway," Dad said. "How do you feel now, Jenna? Up to helping me school a horse?"

The significance of his words did not immediately sink in. I was just back from the hospital where I had been kept overnight with a possible concussion. This morning, after being diagnosed with nothing more serious than a sore head and a rapidly blackening eye, Mom and Dad had brought me back to the farm. Tom too had a few purpling bruises, but right now all I could think of was Cobweb and the little filly I had last seen racing along beside us in flight.

"What's happened to Cobweb and the foal?"

"Don't you worry about it, they're both safe and sound in the stable," Daniel replied.

"Oh, that little filly! She's so cute!" Meg said with delight.

"Mom can't keep away," Kate put in.

"It'll be one spoiled animal," Tom added.

Everyone laughed and began talking about the new addition to the stable, while Meg refilled coffee cups and offered more cake.

"What about Cotebrook?" I said. "Are those awful rumors still going around?"

"Actually, no," Dad said.

Before he could explain the telephone rang. Meg got up to answer it.

"Oh yes, they're both here. One moment, please." She turned to Mom and Dad. "It's for you. A Mr. Carter Harrison?"

"That's the owner of the two-year-old we had in for training," Mom said in a whisper. "Wonder what he wants?"

Meg discreetly said she had things to do and headed off toward the door, gesturing for the others to follow. The room emptied, except for the dogs that sat by the low table, drooling in hopeful anticipation of receiving the one remaining slice of cake on the plate.

Dad took the call. "Mr. Harrison? Marcus Scott here. Good morning."

Dad's face was inscrutable as he listened to what the man had to say. You would have needed to know him very well indeed to detect the tiny sparkle that appeared in his eye as the lengthy monologue ran its course.

"So you would like the filly to return to us?" Dad said, once the owner had finished speaking. "I'll have to have a word with Heather, of course, but I'm sure that won't be a problem. May I get back to you later on today?"

The owner began speaking again. This time Dad's lips quirked into a rare smile.

"Yes, I don't see why not," he responded. "Shall we work on the two-year-old first? Great. I'll call you back this evening. We've actually got a bit of excitement going on here right now – or rather Jenna has. Thanks, Mr. Harrison. 'Bye for now."

He turned to us, his face triumphant. "Carter Harrison is bringing the filly back. What's more, he's sending us others at a later date. He couldn't apologize enough for the 'little glitch', as he called it!"

"Wow!" I said.

"You certainly kept him guessing." Mom sent Dad a sideways look. "Talk it over with Heather indeed!"

"Serve him right for doubting us in the first place. It's always best not to sound too accommodating."

Mom just smiled. "So what else did the great man have to say?"

"Pretty much the same thing we've heard from the rest of the owners. Harrison received an untraceable phone call assuring him that the gossip circulating over Broselake was completely unfounded."

I was mystified. Dad explained.

"It's all turn and turn about, Jenna. For some reason

people have realized they made one huge mistake and are sending their horses back. Amazing, how a tiny seed of doubt can grow all out of proportion, but there it is. We should be back in business by the end of the week."

"Oh, that's great news!"

"I still can't help wondering how it all started," Mom said.

"Let's leave it, Heather. We're back where we were – or will be once those heads are looking out over the stable doors." Dad threw Mom a warm glance.

"It's not like you two to both be away from the yard. Who's keeping an eye on things right now?" I asked.

"Oh, didn't I tell you?" Dad said, sheepish. "We've taken on a student. Once it was obvious that we were back in business Mom and I decided the time had come to bring in some help."

"Male or female?"

"Young guy. His name's Sam."

"What's he like with the horses?"

"Wonderful," Mom said.

We all exchanged a smile. Everything was on track again. It could not have gotten much better.

※ ※ ※

In the box, Cobweb and her daughter stood fetlock deep in straw.

"Hi, you two." I gave Cobweb a hug and got out the mints. The filly, inquisitive, tried to grab the packet. "Hey, cheeky! Stop that. Want one?"

She sniffed, cautious and snorting, and then sampled

the treat, making such a funny face at the strong taste of peppermint that we all laughed.

"She's a star," Kate said.

Even at this young age, Cobweb's neat head and balanced outline were evident in her foal. Her coat had lost most of its foal fluff and was a shade lighter than her mother's. As with Cobweb, the filly had no white markings at all.

"You'll have to get her tested to see who her sire is," Tom said. "Those plains stallions are very sound. You could have a great horse there, Jenna."

"Yes," I said, remembering a stocky gray in my mare's shadow.

Kate giggled. "Love the black eye. You should wear a patch over it, Jenna. Start a trend."

"Oh, shut up," Tom told her lightly. "Or I'll blacken yours to match."

"You wouldn't dare!" Kate sobered. "I was really, really glad to see you two coming out of those woods. Tom was gone for so long, I thought it was the end."

"So did I at one point. That man was the worst. I can see now why Cobweb acted the way she did. Ugh, the way he treated those ponies!"

I shuddered and Tom put his arm around my shoulders and gave a comforting squeeze.

"Don't think about it. It's over. The two ringleaders have been captured and the rest of the gang will be soon be traced." He gave his head a bemused shake. "You've got to hand it to them, they had quite a thing going. I came across their sound system in that defunct burial chamber at Puck's Knowe. It worked off a remote control, sending out freaky wolf cries all over the place. Classic!"

"Not that you ever went along with it," Kate said sweetly.

Tom said she was so right and went to make a fuss over Cobweb. She didn't shy off or even flinch. After a thoughtful pause, she nuzzled Tom's palm in her old affectionate manner and began rubbing her head up and down his body, the way horses do when they are making friends.

"Get a look at this," Tom said, pleased.

"We just did," Kate answered him. "It's fantastic. I get the impression the trouble at Cotebrook has been fixed, too."

"Well, yes," I said. "We still don't know who was behind it all."

"Actually," Tom said. "It was Cerys."

We gaped at him.

"Cerys?" I said in disbelief. "How come?"

"Well, after you two had left on the camping ride, I went to Ravensmoor to meet Cerys as we'd arranged. She was late and I started chatting with Ann Jenkins at the forge. Ann mentioned the gossip that was circulating over Cobweb and the insurance claim. Then Cerys turned up and we went to see this horse she was interested in. It was at the farm where the rally was held."

"What was it like?" Kate wanted to know.

"Oh, great. A nice liver chestnut. Just Cerys's type, or so I thought. Anyway, she tried it out and decided she could do better. The weather was looking iffy so we headed home. Cerys seemed fed up. She said none of the horses she'd seen were what they were cracked up to be. I asked her where else she had been and she said Scotts at Cotebrook."

"She didn't," I said. "Cerys made some inquiries but that's as far as it went. She wanted to jump the waiting list."

Kate snorted. "That's no surprise!"

"Cerys said she wouldn't buy off a yard that wasn't genuine. I asked her what she meant and she just smiled. It was her expression. Sort of… smug." He shrugged. "When I pressed her further it turned out she'd put the word around that Cotebrook wasn't above carrying off a shady deal or two. That's all it takes to make people jump to conclusions. I brought up what Ann Jenkins had told me and asked Cerys if she knew anything about it. She said she did. She seemed proud of it."

"Told you she was a waste of space," Kate muttered.

"What did you do?" I asked Tom.

"Suggested she put things right before the Sport Endurance officials got an earful of what had happened. Cerys didn't want that, not with her dad on the committee. She must have gotten to work right away. A while later I met Ann Jenkins on the road. She pulled up and told me she'd heard on the grapevine that the gossip about Cotebrook was fiction. Not that she'd ever thought otherwise. She'd been shoeing at a yard that had pulled their horses out of Cotebrook and wanted to return them. Good, eh?"

"Very," I said.

"Was that when you set off after us?" Kate asked.

"Yes. I thought Jenna would want to hear the good news. I wasn't too happy about what was going on out there, either."

We knew the rest. Tom had thrown some camping gear together and set off to catch up to us. The flash floods at Ravensmoor had delayed him, as he'd had to take the longer route. The light I had seen at Puck's Knowe was Tom arriving there. After seeing the "ghostly" rider, he had investigated the Neolithic burial chamber and discovered a set of dress up clothes daubed with phosphorescent paint like those at the rustlers' base.

"It was the sound system that put me onto their game," Tom said. "The setup was far too sophisticated to be an innocent prank. I guessed you could have ridden into a trap, and I couldn't go after you fast enough."

"I had a feeling we were being followed," I said.

"You and your intuitions!" Kate rolled her eyes despairingly.

Tom caught my glance. He accepted there was more to it than I was prepared to say, but being Tom he was not going to pry.

We had heard that the yearlings that were going to be exported were now being sorted out and delivered to their rightful owners. Nobody would ever know what had happened to the previous rustling assignments but, as Kate pointed out, we just had to hope that the ponies had ultimately all found good homes. It appeared that the owners of the rescued yearlings were pulling together some sort of reward, and Kate's portion was going toward a top-flight security system for Broselake.

There were still a few loose ends to tie up. I couldn't wait to see Harriet Newby's reaction when she learned what had happened, and Gary Robinson and the endurance club members would be interested too.

Tom said, "Dad was making noises about putting the champagne on ice to wet the filly's head. Have you thought of a name for her, Jenna?"

"Sneezy?" Kate suggested.

"No!" I said, laughing. "I'm calling her Mani. Spirit of Mani officially."

I ran my hand along the smooth, unblemished crest of Cobweb's neck, thinking of that strange symbol and how it had puzzled and frightened me. It had now vanished completely, but what else could it have been but a plea for help? The moon goddess, outraged at having her name usurped by a gang of freaky horse rustlers, had sent the mark knowing I would be able to feel the vibes and hoping I would get in touch, so that the thieves might be exposed and an end would be put to the misuse of her name. She had sent the midnight hoofbeats and the stallion too, doing all she could do alert me. I remembered the images in the stable after touching the symbol – the robed figure, the scene with a line of trees edging the high plain. I should have realized that all the while she had been nudging me toward the rustlers' hideout, but at the time I had been too fogged with fear and self-doubt to see it.

Had she sent the storm as well? It would have been within her power. The more I thought about it, the more probable it seemed.

I had to wonder if Mani had used the moon and horse mark on previous occasions with other mares, and failed to make contact until now. It was likely. At least I, with that uncanny sixth sense that Gran called a gift, had picked up on the messages. And I couldn't help feeling that in some kindly way the moon goddess had wanted to lead me to Cobweb's foal, so that mother and foal might be reunited.

I knew I was no longer afraid of myself. Accept and move on had been Gran's advice, and I could now do that. Earlier, I had sent Gran an e-mail.

Everything fine. Talk soon. Love, Jenna.

In the next box Zaide gave a low, disgruntled whicker.

"She's feeling neglected," Kate said. "I'd better make a fuss or she'll never speak to me again."

When Kate had left, Tom looked at me seriously.

"You were brave back there in the woods. Most girls would have run for it while they had the chance."

"I wasn't brave at all," I said. "I was completely freaked out."

"You were terrific. If you hadn't turned back there's no saying how things might have ended. Thanks, Jenna."

His eyes were very blue in the dimness of the stable and my heart gave an odd little leap. He seemed about to say more, but first there was something I had to know.

"Tom, when that guy had you pinned down and I yelled for help, what did you see?"

Tom took a moment to consider. "It was more what I heard. A din like a stallion making a war charge, the way they once did in battle?" He paused, frowning. "I may have seen something too. It was… oh, I don't know. Whatever, it gave us the break we needed."

He smiled down at me. "Jenna, there's something I want to ask you. Would you like to go to the jazz club sometime? And don't give me any of that garbage about not being good enough. You've got a great vocal range. I know you can do it."

I hesitated, but only for a moment. "OK, I'll give it a try."

"Great," Tom said.

"I know what I'm spending my reward money on too. A flute. I wouldn't mind learning to play one."

"Gets better," Tom said.

He opened the stable door and, leaving Cobweb with her daughter, we went out into the sunshine. Kate, stuffing Zaide with slices of carrot in the adjoining box, came to join us.

"Jenna's promised to sing at the gigs," Tom told her.

"Cool!" was all Kate said.

Smiling, the three of us linked arms and set off across the farmyard, heading for the house where our folks waited.